RYOHGO
NARITA

ILLUSTRATION BY
SUZUHITO YASUDA

DURARARA!!

DRRR!!

SH1

Himeka Tatsugami

"As long as the Headless Rider exists, I can't change, and neither can this city."

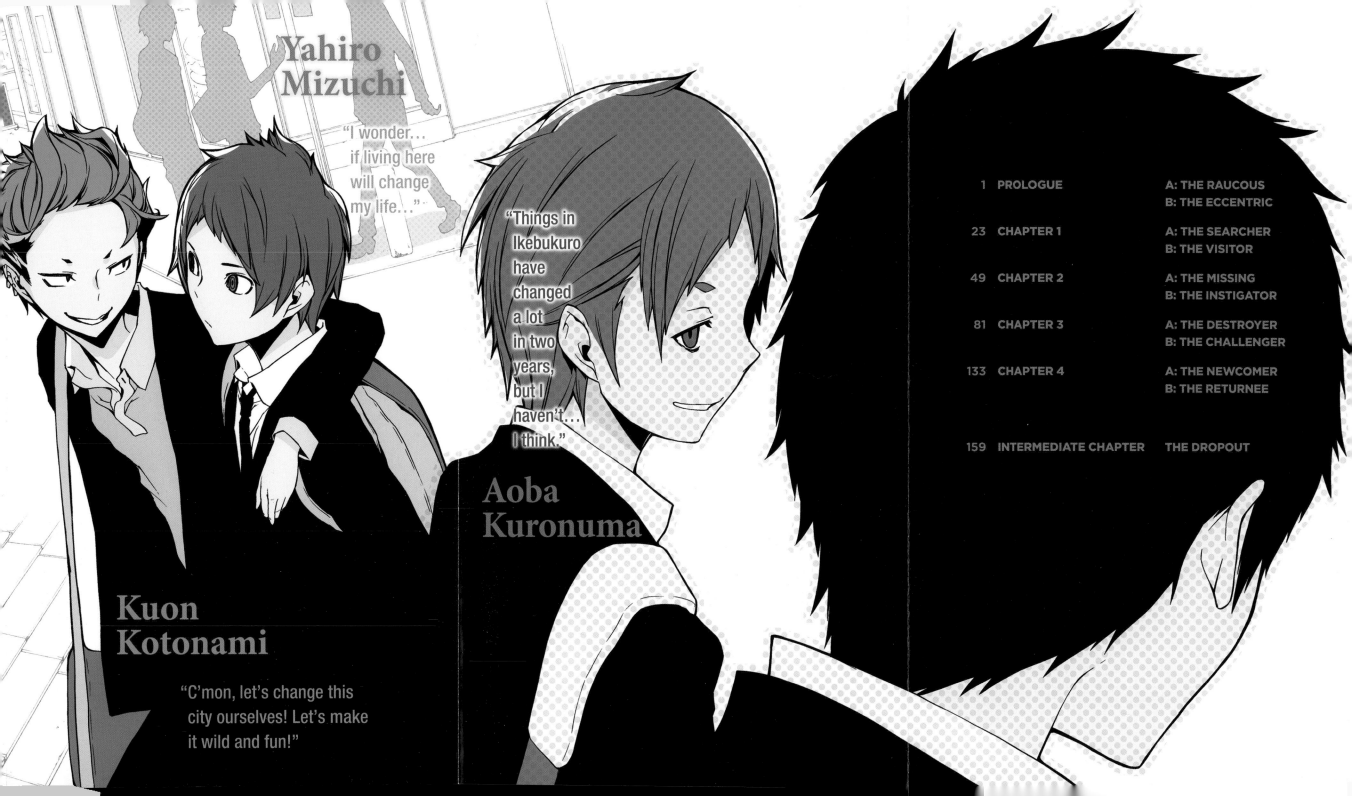

Yahiro Mizuchi

"I wonder… if living here will change my life…"

Aoba Kuronuma

"Things in Ikebukuro have changed a lot in two years, but I haven't… I think."

Kuon Kotonami

"C'mon, let's change this city ourselves! Let's make it wild and fun!"

1	PROLOGUE	A: THE RAUCOUS
		B: THE ECCENTRIC
23	CHAPTER 1	A: THE SEARCHER
		B: THE VISITOR
49	CHAPTER 2	A: THE MISSING
		B: THE INSTIGATOR
81	CHAPTER 3	A: THE DESTROYER
		B: THE CHALLENGER
133	CHAPTER 4	A: THE NEWCOMER
		B: THE RETURNEE
159	INTERMEDIATE CHAPTER	THE DROPOUT

VOLUME 1

Ryohgo Narita
ILLUSTRATION BY **Suzuhito Yasuda**

NEW YORK

Durarara!! SH, Vol. 1
Ryohgo Narita

Translation by Stephen Paul
Yen On edition edited by Carly Smith & Yen Press Editorial
Cover art by Suzuhito Yasuda

This book is a work of fiction. Names, characters, places, and incidents are the product of the author's imagination or are used fictitiously. Any resemblance to actual events, locales, or persons, living or dead, is coincidental.

DURARARA!!SH Vol. 1
©Ryohgo Narita 2014
Edited by Dengeki Bunko
First published in Japan in 2014 by KADOKAWA CORPORATION, Tokyo.
English translation rights arranged with KADOKAWA CORPORATION, Tokyo,
through TUTTLE-MORI AGENCY, INC., Tokyo.

English translation © 2021 by Yen Press, LLC

Yen On
150 West 30th Street, 19th Floor
New York, NY 10001

Visit us at yenpress.com
facebook.com/yenpress
twitter.com/yenpress
yenpress.tumblr.com
instagram.com/yenpress

First Yen On Edition: May 2021

Yen On is an imprint of Yen Press, LLC.
The Yen On name and logo are trademarks of Yen Press, LLC.

The publisher is not responsible for websites (or their content) that are not owned by the publisher.

Library of Congress Cataloging-in-Publication Data
Names: Narita, Ryōgo, 1980- author. | Yasuda, Suzuhito, illustrator. |
Paul, Stephen (Translator), translator.
Title: Durarara!! SH / Ryohgo Narita ; illustration by Suzuhito Yasuda ;
translation by Stephen Paul.
Other titles: Durarara!! (Light novel). English
Description: First Yen On edition. | New York : Yen On, 2021.
Identifiers: LCCN 2021009783 | ISBN 9781975322779
(v. 1 ; trade paperback)
Subjects: CYAC: Fantasy. | Tokyo (Japan)—Fiction.
Classification: LCC PZ7.1.N37 Dur 2021 | DDC [Fic]—dc23
LC record available at https://lccn.loc.gov/2021009783

ISBNs: 978-1-9753-2277-9 (paperback)
978-1-9753-2278-6 (ebook)

1 3 5 7 9 10 8 6 4 2

LSC-C

Printed in the United States of America

dasoku ("snake legs")

   adj., Taken from the ancient Chinese state of Chu, where in a race to paint a snake, the fastest artist got carried away and drew legs, thus losing the contest ("Strategies of Qi," *Strategies of the Warring States*). Something superfluous or unnecessary.

   —*Digital Daijisen* dictionary © Shogakukan Inc.,
      1995, 1998, 2012

This is a superfluous tale.

The Headless Rider, the colorless street gang, a cursed sword that slashes humanity because of an abundance of love—these strange and eerie monsters left scars on the city of Ikebukuro.

The people of this city imagined, fantasized, and in some cases even loved these monsters—creating their urban legends that are passed on through the streets.

And now the legs of the snake have been added to that completed portrait.

Some might call this an unnecessary story.

A superfluous detail added to the massive snake that is an urban legend.

However, it is vital to remember this: The front legs of the snake can evolve into arms, and if they should grow claws that seize all, the snake has the potential to become a dragon.

PROLOGUE A
The Raucous

"You monster."

Before he graduated middle school, the boy had heard these words countless times.

There was a remote hot springs town in the mountains of Akita Prefecture—a place prized for its underrated natural baths and blessed with visitors year-round—but it was unable to keep up with steady depopulation and slowly faded away into obscurity.

The boy was born here fifteen years ago. Supposedly, anyway—there was a lack of concrete information in that regard.

He was found at the doorstep of a hot springs inn, an infant wrapped in a blanket, just clipped from the umbilical cord.

An elderly woman who ran the inn took in the baby, raising him as a foster child by her daughter's family. He was raised with a proper amount of love and beautiful surroundings. He grew up in what felt like no time at all.

But before his heart and soul could grow healthy and strong as well, he suffered the interference of others.

It's a story that can be found anywhere. People were jealous of the child being fostered by one of the wealthier families in town and tried to hurt him. Emotionally, and perhaps even physically.

That was how the village learned he was different.

*   *   *

He was a new student in elementary school when one boy, five years older and quite large for his age, picked a fight with him. This boy had a reputation for being a nasty troublemaker, and one day, he chose to make the newcomer his target.

At this point, the little boy did not understand that he was a foster child, nor even what those words were supposed to mean.

But when the insults didn't have the intended effect, the older boy turned to more drastic means. He punched the child, then grabbed his collar. Everyone knew what kind of bullying this would turn out to be.

And in fact, the fight that resulted was over quickly.

But not in a way anyone expected.

That was the moment he first exhibited his special power.

He hadn't been trained in some way to prepare for this. He didn't have flesh like steel or the freakish strength necessary to lift a vending machine with one hand.

But he did have one thing: something like an extra sense.

Some carnivorous animals are born knowing how to bring down their prey; in the same way, as soon as the older boy grabbed the younger's collar, the child turned that aggression back upon him.

He grabbed his enemy's ears, yanking them downward.

The bully let go and crouched to create less leverage for pulling, his instincts screaming that his ears were going to be ripped off. Now it was even easier for the six-year-old to head-butt him on the bridge of his nose.

The child did not *know* how to do this, of course. He simply tried to hit his opponent with the hardest part of his body as quickly as possible. Not that it was normal for a child so young to possess that instinct at all.

Furthermore, he was too young to understand concepts like *mercy* or *restraint*.

If the boy's personality were to be described as succinctly as possible, it would distill into one word.

Cowardice.

He was a coward, and thus he hated being afraid.

That was all it came down to.

He was twice as sensitive to fear as the average person and twice as desperate to avoid it.

So the combination of his cowardice and his "talent" gave birth to a monster.

A much older boy threatening him and yelling about something he didn't understand created enough fear to force him to respond in equal measure.

Must avoid fear.

Must eliminate it.

Following his instincts, the boy kicked and kicked at the older child, who was now huddled on the ground.

He aimed right for the face.

Using the tip of his toes, he crushed the fingers that tried to protect the bully's features.

Even when the blood seeped through those fingers to drip onto the ground, he did not hesitate.

On and on and on, he attacked without stopping.

From that point on, the boy was feared by those around him.

Immediately following that incident, he avoided consequences because everyone saw the older boy attack him first; plus, he was the child of a prominent family in town. However, that was just the start of the strain upon his life.

Although, in a sense, this was also when the strain was lifted from him, as he lived in accordance with his abilities.

The village population might have been dwindling over the years, but there were still people who wanted to mess with the kid.

There were other older boys who wanted revenge for their friend and decided to teach this little upstart a lesson. Some of them were even in middle school. Once a gang like that jumped him, he wouldn't stand a chance.

Or so they thought.

The first one of them landed a punch and straddled the new student—who then promptly thrust a finger in his attacker's eye.

He didn't fully gouge it, but as soon as the other boys saw the blood from their friend's eye and heard his screams, they were stunned.

The little six-year-old picked up a nearby rock and moved to further incapacitate the screaming boy who was rolling on the ground.

And when the rest of the group saw the intense, feverish look in the child's eyes, they all had the same thought: *Whatever this kid is, he's not like us. He's something else.*

He was merely a young boy, more than a head shorter than they were and well before his growth spurt.

But to them, he fought as fiercely as any wolf or bear.

If they had regrouped at once and several attacked the boy at a time, they would have stood a chance of winning. They weren't some combat-ready group of delinquents or bikers, though. It was too much to ask of a rabble of elementary and middle school boys who thought they were tough.

They knew the next person to attack would suffer the same fate.

The sight of their friend getting his teeth broken by a rock kept them nailed in place.

This time, he was reported as engaging in excessive self-defense, and despite being only six years old, the boy had to answer to the police, who contacted a child welfare agency.

After that, no one in the town dared attack the boy until he started middle school. Other people from the wider region outside the town, having heard rumors from the local punks, began to check in and mess with him.

Their reasoning was simple.

All those older boys had grown up and left for other areas, where they made new friends and enemies—and at a certain point, some of them let slip the name of the little boy who had nearly killed them years ago.

The trauma of their past had added extra details to the story as it existed in their memory. They spoke of the "six-year-old who ripped a kid's ears off, then fought a group of ten without fear and broke all of one guy's ribs with a rock."

And then, out of curiosity and for their own amusement, those delinquents from other areas tried their luck, too.

They found out that, in the same way stories often grow legs of their own, the boy had also grown quite a lot in the years since.

*   *   *

"Damn monster."

Soon after the boy had started middle school, he heard those venomous words from some half-dead sucker.

At this point, the boy couldn't remember the first time he'd heard that word.

"You monster."

"Monster."

"You're a monster."

They came to avenge their friends.

They came to show off and build legends of their own prowess.

All kinds of cocky fighters looking to test their mettle came to his town.

The boy defeated all of them—only because he was afraid.

He was just trying to live a normal life; yet, he was terrorized by constant threats and hostility that he did not deserve.

So he began to work out. He wanted to protect himself from the regular visits of terror.

In the meantime, the stories of his ability spread so far that ruffians began coming from other prefectures just to challenge him.

He spent his days in combat. Strengthening himself to defeat his fears.

And that was how his innate talent was augmented with experience and effort.

Nothing about this was fair.

He didn't pick any of these fights. It was everyone else who antagonized him, yet they called *him* an inhuman monster after they'd lost.

By the time he was in eighth grade and fifteen years old, he had given up on everything.

At this point in his life, he knew he was an orphan.

While he had nothing but gratitude for the parents who raised him, he had lost all hope for the world at large.

As long as people called him a monster, his life would never be normal.

This is what life and human society were like.

It was cruel to him—cruel enough to make a fifteen-year-old boy feel this way.

Even after these fights, the boy's family did not abandon him. Because all the delinquents attacking him had metal pipes and knives, the police labeled his actions self-defense, which helped him avoid any trips to juvenile detention.

That, however, did not stop the endless deluge of hatred and fear he lived within.

If anything, the kindness of his family isolated him further.

Being called a monster made him a burden on his ordinary, loving family. He felt guilty for holding them down.

He was trapped in a vicious cycle, no longer hopeful for the world but not plunged into despair, either. His life felt like it had no proper substance.

He assumed this was just going to be the state of things for the rest of his years.

Until a major turning point arrived.

One day, at the end of summer, a visitor from Tokyo arrived at their village.

The man had come to see the famous Omagari fireworks show and stopped at the little town to enjoy its hot springs before returning home.

He stayed at the biggest hot spring in the town, where he ended up witnessing a fight between the boy and his aggressors.

The visitor watched this brutal melee with great interest. When it was over, he smiled and spared a word for the boy.

"It's always nice to see young folks being lively."

The boy looked skeptical.

Tourists had witnessed his fights on several occasions, but people had only ever been afraid of him. Nobody had ever chuckled with delight before.

The boy stood among the bruised and bloodied ruffians on the ground. The tourist continued, "When you're young and overflowing with energy, it's good to live true to your human instincts." The man didn't seem to have an inkling of morals about him.

The boy asked, "What human instincts? Do I look human to you?"

The traveler replied, "Those are odd things to ask. If you're not human, then what *are* you?" He grinned warmly. "Yes, you're a powerful fighter, but that just means you're a person who happens to be good at fighting. There are plenty of people in the world who are far less human than you. And there are real inhuman creatures, too."

The boy was suspicious. This man said some very strange things.

But he didn't seem like he was lying.

At the very least, the boy was taken aback that this man could have witnessed the fight and call him "human."

What sort of things had this traveler seen in his life?

As the man turned to leave, the boy blurted out, "Where are you from?"

The tourist turned back and beamed.

"Ikebukuro."

He'd heard that name before.

It was one of the famous areas in Tokyo, but the boy had barely traveled beyond the limits of his little village. It was only a name he'd heard, nothing more.

Curious, he booted up the smartphone he rarely ever used and typed "Ikebukuro" into the search bar.

It did not take long before he started seeing certain information about this far-off place: vivid video footage of a headless being and a man throwing a vending machine.

He held his breath and tore through all the information he could find, as if he were possessed.

The Headless Rider.

The mysterious bartender.

The Dollars.

The street slasher.

All these keywords seemed like things out of a comic book, but there they were, right on the screen of his phone.

He could feel his heart beating faster.

All along, he'd accepted loneliness—that he was a monster and nothing more. Now a new world was opening before his eyes.

The boy lived and breathed combat. But through the tiny window of his smartphone, he saw the whole wide world.

And yes, it was frightening.

The cowardice that made the boy a monster had calmed somewhat as he grew up, but it was still a part of him.

The Headless Rider was terrifying.

The man who threw vending machines around was terrifying.

The slasher was terrifying.

A gang made up of hundreds of people was terrifying.

But all these shocks to his system stimulated his mind.

For once, curiosity outweighed the fear.

Normally, he would be terrified of a headless being roaming the city.

He would never, ever want to visit Ikebukuro.

However, now he was becoming aware of his true feelings.

If anything, the most frightening thing of all would be to give up on the idea that the world could be anything different—to live and die alone as a monster.

Eventually, the information from that tiny little window wasn't enough for him anymore.

When it came time to decide his future path in life, he went to his foster parents and decided to speak his true desires aloud.

All the fighting was something that happened *to* him, not something he sought out, but there was no denying its negative effect on his family.

Some angry losers had once tried to get back at him by lighting the inn on fire, which ended up getting the police involved. Either out of guilt for causing that or out of indebtedness that they didn't abandon him following the incident, the boy had never truly expressed his most selfish desires to them.

His resignation toward the world and the rigors of all that fighting hardened him into a very upstanding person. He had never begged his parents or grandparents for anything.

And now, for the very first time since his initial fight in elementary school, he was asking what his heart wanted.

*　　*　　*

I want to go to high school in Tokyo—in Ikebukuro.

It came out of nowhere to his parents. They were stunned.

But the boy was proactively admitting that he wanted to learn more. The grandmother of the family, who had final say as owner of the inn, said, "C'mere, you. Siddan there."

He obeyed, and she stared him in the eyes and drawled in her thick Akita accent, "You were ta timidest boya ever saw...an' look how grown, yuh nah?"

It didn't happen right away, but ultimately his grandmother's vote of sympathy swayed the decision.

And that was how the boy they called a monster came to Ikebukuro.

He was ready to face the world he'd given up on.

He was there to meet the *true* monsters he'd never seen before.

The boy's name was Yahiro Mizuchi.

He didn't know what he would see in the days ahead.

Who was the cowardly monster going to meet on the streets of Ikebukuro?

What would he achieve—or not achieve?

No one could say, but one thing was certain:

The city was not going to resist anyone who came to its borders, no matter who they were.

A year and a half had passed since the demise of the Dollars.

Ikebukuro was ready to welcome a new breeze.

PROLOGUE B
The Eccentric

A city is constantly changing, so long as people continue living in it.

Ikebukuro was no exception. Because it was a place full of people, the city's atmosphere was always evolving, from trends coming and going to subtle economic and social fluctuations.

But cities and people are one organism, by nature.

People can change a city, and people change themselves to fit in with the city.

This process can be growth or regression or something else entirely—but ultimately, the result of this change is something that belongs to each individual.

"I can't believe we're third-years already. Have you been thinking about your future plans, Kuru?" asked a girl walking along the busy shopping street leading from Ikebukuro Station to the Sunshine building, commonly known as Sixtieth Floor Street. Her conversation partner's face looked identical.

"…Yeah…" [Affirmative.]

The elder of the two sisters had a voice as quiet as an insect's whisper.

"Urgh. Kuru, you're such a Goody Two-shoes. I'm, like, maybe I should just be a bum and hang around not getting a job. You can graduate, get a job, and support me, Kuru!"

"…No…" [Pain in the butt.]

They were identical twins—but only as far as their faces were concerned.

The younger twin, Mairu Orihara, wore glasses and had her long hair tied into braids. The style was usually associated with mature honor students, but her personality was active and upbeat, suggesting she was the type to speak before she thought.

The elder twin, Kururi Orihara, had a tomboyish appearance, but she was almost deathly quiet in her mannerisms. She was more like an antique doll.

The contrasting fashions were not a natural evolution of their individuality, either.

When they were children, they intentionally chose to have totally opposing personalities and interests.

Twins are a symbol of perfection because we can each account for what the other lacks, they thought. So they drew random lots to ensure they each covered different aspects, determining their future development from childhood onward.

Now they would know how they should live their lives. And if there was any problem for either sister, they would work together to solve it.

It might have started as a childish flight of fancy, but that was, in fact, how they grew up.

About the only interest they shared in common was an obsession with the handsome young actor Yuuhei Hanejima. That and their love for each other.

The twins were some of the more well-known characters in this city.

They were students at Raira Academy, a high school in Ikebukuro, and they were enjoying their spring vacation by idling away the time until it was nearly over.

"I can't believe we're going to be seniors. It passed so quickly. We were just first-years, and now we're going to be in our third year of school. It feels like it's only been like three months."

"...Light..." [It's been so fast.]

"But things have changed around town so much. When those nerdy stores like Animate and Toranoana opened new spots or changed locations, Karisawa and her friends went crazy. And there are plenty of other new businesses," Mairu said, her braids swaying as she craned her neck to look around. "But then again, there are some things that never change. Like that Cinema Sunshine over there, and the arcade, and..."

She trailed off. There was a familiar face near the entrance of the video game arcade that shared a wall with the movie theater.

"Oh, look, Kuru. Aocchi's over there. He's with Yoshikiri and his other friends."

Kururi followed her sister's gaze and saw Aoba Kuronuma, a boy from their school. Obviously, he wasn't in his school uniform, since they were on vacation, and so the vibe he gave off was much different from at school.

"You'll be a senior, too, Aobacchi. You were very childish when we first met, but now you're a bit taller," said Mairu wistfully, striding with purpose toward the group of boys.

Without missing a beat, she smashed the top of Aoba's head with a karate chop.

"Yeow!"

"Yoo-hoo! What's up, Aocchi? You still alive?"

"Mairu...? What kind of greeting is that?" Aoba groaned with an exhausted sigh.

She grinned and hissed with laughter. "Look, I haven't seen you in a while, Aocchi. I was worried that you might've gotten yourself in hot water and died. That's the kind of thing you'd do."

"Wow, you have some intense preconceptions of me," replied Aoba, his cheek twitching.

She continued, "But you *are* mixed up in some danger, right? You were getting into it with Dragon Zombie recently, weren't you?"

"...You always have your ear to the ground."

Aoba Kuronuma was the central figure of a group of delinquents known as the Blue Squares.

They had once been a street gang recognized by their blue bandannas and ski masks, but their color theme was more reserved now. They weren't attempting to stand out the way they did before.

In fact, this boy did not look like a street tough in the least. Mairu chattered on.

"Actually, I'm more out of the loop than I used to be. My dear brother, Iza, up and disappeared, and Namie went to the States. About the only people I can hit up for the latest news are the people at Rakuei Gym these days."

"And in any case, none of it has to do with you." Aoba shrugged.

Kururi leaned close to his ear and whispered, "...Negative...alone... death..." [You can't just go off on your own and die.]

"Aaah!!" he yelped.

She pressed her forehead against his shoulder and gave him a little smile.

"...!" Aoba's mouth quavered, and his cheeks went red. Then he said, "Don't threaten me like that," and turned away.

But that only put him face-to-face with one of his friends, whose cheeks were twitching with obvious disgust.

"Wh-what, Yoshikiri?"

"I can't believe you... Getting all sappy with these cute girls right in the open like this... These cute—! Girls—!" said the boy, who was an entire head taller than Aoba. He put a hand on the back of Aoba's neck. "I'll kill you! One less guy means better chances for the rest of us!"

"Well, it's not gonna help *your* chances, Yoshikiri... *Urrrgl—!* I give! I give! I give!" Aoba gurgled, his face turning purple. The other boys laughed uproariously.

Once he was getting to a somewhat distressing color, another boy popped out from farther back in the arcade. Alarmed, he cried out, "Hey! Yoshikiri, what are you doing to Kuronuma?!"

This boy looked younger than the rest of them, and it took his full effort to pry Yoshikiri off Aoba's neck.

"Let go of me, Kotonami! If I kill him, girls will like me!"

"Of course they're not going to like you, Yoshikiri!"

"...What?"

"Ah!"

Yoshikiri let go of Aoba's neck and turned, a vein pulsing at his temple. Now his hands were reaching for this younger boy, and he soon had his victim in a cobra twist, locking all his joints.

"What is it with you pretty boys and your death wishes? Huh?!"

"Aaaah! I give! I give! I give!"

*   *   *

Several minutes later, after an arcade employee came along to scold Yoshikiri, the boy was free. He rubbed the sore parts all over his body and asked Aoba, "Are those pretty twins your girlfriends, Kuronuma?"

"No!" shouted Yoshikiri instantaneously, but Aoba ignored him.

"No...they're not my girlfriends, they're more like...regular friends," he claimed brusquely, but that only put a mischievous grin on Mairu's lips.

"Right, right. We're friends. Me and Kuru have only kissed Aocchi, nothing more than that."

"H-hey!" Aoba tried to interject, but it was too late to stop Yoshikiri.

"Rrraaaaahhh! I'll kill you! You kiss them, then claim they're just friends?! *Both* of them?! I guess that's the kind of confidence a true winner has, then! By the power vested in me by the other guys in the world, I'm gonna kill... Hey, what do you think you're doing?! Let go o' me, dammit!"

Worried that he was going to get permanently banned from the arcade, the other guys in the group held Yoshikiri down and dragged him away to some other location in town.

That left Aoba behind to exhale with exhaustion. He went ahead and introduced the younger boy to the girls.

"Um, these two girls are from my school. Kururi and Mairu Ori-hara. As you can see—well, they're not *totally* identical, but their faces sure are—they're twins."

Then, for the sisters' benefit, he introduced the younger boy. "This is Kotonami. He's a younger friend of ours who will be joining Raira this year."

"Hi, I'm Kuon Kotonami."

"Kuon? That's kind of a cool name."

"You think so? Thanks," he said with a shrug and a grin.

Mairu gave him a piercing examination. "In fact, you're pretty funky overall. Were you really in middle school a few months ago?"

It was a rather frank assessment, but she couldn't be blamed for feeling that way. He did not at all look like a boy who had just graduated middle school.

His hair was cut short around his ears, with little notches shaved into the sides, while the rest of it was grown out longer and dyed a shocking tint of green. He sported wild earrings all along his ears, which in combination with his hairstyle suggested a strong streak of self-expression.

His features were handsome enough, but the loud accessories were destined to take up most of the first impression. Mairu's eyes were flashing with fascination; he looked like the most eye-catching member of a visual kei rock band.

But then Aoba smirked and showed her his phone. "This is what he looked like last month."

"H-hey, Kuronuma! No fai…"

Kuon tried to snatch the phone, but Mairu ducked past him and lifted it right out of Aoba's hand.

The picture on the screen was of a perfect honor student with black hair in a bob cut and glasses to boot. Mairu clutched her sides and roared with laughter. Even Kururi shivered as she tried to control the giggles threatening to burst out of her.

"Ah-ha-ha-ha-ha-ha-ha! This is amazing! So you're making your big social debut in high school, huh?! Or are you starting up a visual kei band?"

"…Relax…normal…" [It's fine; you look good.]

Kuon's face turned red, and he balled his hands into fists that he shook up and down. "Aaaaaah! That was messed up, Kuronuma! This is terrorism! It's bullying! This is what a mother-in-law does to the new wife!"

"It's fine. This is the easiest way to introduce you." Aoba cackled.

Mairu laughed along with him—until she abruptly composed herself, still smiling, and asked, "But your appearance is the only thing you're changing for high school, right?"

"Huh?"

"I mean, if you know Aocchi, and you're still hanging out with him now, then you must have *always* been messed up and broken and kinda sick… Am I wrong?"

"…"

The boys had no response to that.

It wasn't that Mairu had come to that conclusion because she was cracked in the head or anything like that. Anyone who was familiar with Aoba Kuronuma and the Blue Squares would have the same expectation.

In contrast to his looks, Aoba Kuronuma had a dark and twisted personality. He wouldn't think twice about crushing another person for his personal pleasure and that of his friends.

He had already built the core of the Blue Squares in his junior high years, but he chose not to stand in the limelight—instead, he orchestrated those older than he was, even his own brother, to run the operation publicly, so he could lurk in the background as the puppet master.

There was no way anyone like him would hang out with some random middle school kid who looked up to tough gangsters.

There had to be something else behind it.

Anyone who was familiar with Aoba's true nature would eventually reach this conclusion.

But Mairu's ability to say that out loud in his presence indicated that she was something of a character herself.

After a pause, Kuon managed to put on a new kind of smile, something tinged with coldness, and murmured, "Your girlfriend is very interesting, sir."

"I told you, she's not my girlfriend. If I was going to have a relationship with either of them, it would definitely be Kururi…"

"Really?! You're going to say that in front of me, Aocchi?! Where is your common sense, boy?!" Mairu screeched. Kururi did not seem moved in one way or the other.

Kuon decided to butt out of the situation between his upperclassmen and waved a hand. "Well, I don't want to get in the way, so I'll go help calm down Yoshikiri, I guess."

"Hey, wait. I told you not to get the wrong idea…"

"Enjoy your life, Kuronuma, sir," the younger boy said blithely, leaving the scene.

Aoba could only sigh. He looked to Kururi and Mairu, his expression serious. "Listen, for your own sake, I don't think you should get involved with him."

"What? That's hypocritical. You seem to know him plenty well, Aocchi."

"Well…I dunno; he's just *weird*…," Aoba mumbled vaguely. But then he steeled himself and forged ahead with an explanation. "He might dress flashy, but his entrance exam scores were at the top in Raira."

"What? Really?! He's a genius! He's a professor!"

"...Shock..." [Amazing.]

"Yeah. They asked him to give the speech for the incoming class. But he shows up dressed like that, right? So they had to pivot to somebody else at the last minute when they saw him," Aoba said, averting his eyes.

Mairu inquired, "So why's a boy like that hanging out with you guys?"

"Don't make it sound like we're just a bunch of idiots... Anyway, we kind of have a give-and-take relationship... Basically, he's a valuable source of income for us."

"What?! He's your money tree?!"

"Don't say it like that." Aoba grimaced.

But she grabbed him by the collar with both hands and shook him. "Hey! Are you saying he's from a superrich family, and you guys are shaking him down for money?!"

"...Wicked..." [That's so mean.]

"N...no! No, it's not like that! I swear!"

"Then what *is* it like?" Mairu said. She stopped shaking Aoba, who coughed and cleared his throat.

"He's got his own unique way of making money. We help him and get a part of the cut. Basically, we're working jobs at a business he operates, I guess. Not that it's a store or anything like that."

"You don't mean producing drugs...or growing marijuana, or..."

"No, no, no, nothing like that! It's just on this side of legal. I think..."

"Ohhhh! I get it! I know what it is!" Mairu exclaimed, but Aoba quickly cut her off.

"And it's not some kind of synthetic cannabis or other quasi-legal substance!"

"Awww."

"Shouldn't you be relieved, not disappointed...?" he grumbled, annoyed.

Kururi approached and asked, "...What...act...?" [What kind of job is it?]

"Well, I can't explain it so easily..."

"...Answer...?" [Will you tell me?]

"..."

Aoba relented, breaking under Kururi's quiet pressure, and sighed yet again. "I just can't keep up my front around you two. It's something about you... But anyway, it's kind of an odd jobs service. We might do stuff that resembles newspaper delivery or faking events for TV programs, causing uproars around town—things like that."

"Um...how does that make you money?"

"...He's got connections that allow him to turn these things into money. And I've got the details on his biggest pipeline. It doesn't come up for him very often is the thing."

"Pipeline?" repeated Mairu, who was having trouble visualizing Kuon's "unique way of making money."

Aoba smirked and said, "You already know the answer."

"?"

"The Headless Rider."

"!"

That familiar title caused Kururi and Mairu to share a look.

"Kuon's a real eccentric, see. He wants to turn the Headless Rider's existence itself into money. Not in a bounty hunter kind of way."

"Turn the Headless Rider into money?! What does that mean?!"

"...Not *just* the Headless Rider," said Aoba. The image of his underclassman's face put a very pleased twist into his lips. "He's a real snake."

"Snake?" Mairu repeated. So Aoba went on.

"He wants to swallow Ikebukuro whole, himself included."

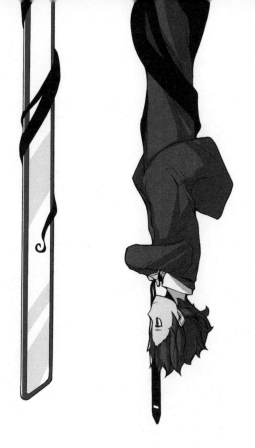

CHAPTER 1

CHAPTER 1 A
The Searcher

An excerpt from a report by Aya Tatsugami, junior reporter for Tokyo Warrior

There is a legend in Ikebukuro of a Headless Rider.

However, the origin of the actual urban legend of the Headless Rider does not hail from Ikebukuro.

There is no particular location that serves as the source of the legend. The rumors began to spread from places all over the country.

Originally, the story appeared as the vengeful spirit of a biker who was decapitated by a wire strung across the street, giving it many aspects of other ghost stories. The gruesome image of accidental beheading creating a ghost could certainly have popped up in disparate locations given the right circumstances, thanks to its lurid nature.

But the version of the legend found in Ikebukuro has a different nature.

If anything, it's closer to a cryptid, like the famous Loch Ness Monster or yeti.

For one thing, the Headless Rider here does not require some ghostly sixth sense (if such a thing can be argued to exist) in order to perceive. Anyone and everyone is capable of sensing its presence.

It became known to people all over the country when it was caught clearly on TV news cameras.

Ordinarily, this sort of thing would be derided as a cheap TV stunt, but in this case, there were too many witnesses.

The Headless Rider has been seen in the Ikebukuro area going back over twenty years, in fact, but photographic evidence of the rider only came about as cell phones with cameras became more widespread.

People in the media would buy the images originally out of curiosity, but at this point, there is such a flood of evidence online that they might as well be cat or dog photos for how easy it is to find them.

Even then, if you remove people who have actually seen the rider in Ikebukuro, public belief in a being that rides around the city without a head is only about fifty-fifty.

The first time I saw it, I thought it was just some camera trick set up by the TV station, too.

The footage was shown live during a police segment on the news, so you might consider the entire thing to have been a setup. I shared that opinion, assuming that it was something only slightly fancier than the many fake photographs found all over the Internet.

But then I actually encountered it myself in Ikebukuro.

A motorcycle that rides without a sound and reflects no light.

The being sitting atop it wore a helmet, preventing me from determining if there was truly a head underneath or not. But that did not matter to me. The fact that it raced by at astonishing speed without so much as a hint of engine noise was plenty to convince me of its otherworldly nature.

And to add to that, while the police motorcycles gave apparent chase, the Headless Rider extended something black that I can only describe as shadow from its body, creating an obsidian path upon which it could travel.

To be quite frank, after the impossible sight of a silent motorcycle traveling up a route that it created out of itself, the question of whether the Headless Rider was truly headless or not seemed like the least pertinent bit of information.

Ever since, I have been following the Headless Rider.

And my pursuit has put me in possession of a number of fascinating facts.

A reporter from Daioh TV attempted to interview the rider on the street, at which point it used an electronic device to communicate.

On that footage, the motorcycle without headlights can be seen transforming into a headless horse. For this reason, commenters online speculated that the Headless Rider might actually be a dullahan.

A dullahan is a type of fairy stemming from Irish tradition, a being that comes to warn those who are soon to die of their impending demise.

It is supposed to carry its own head under its arm, but the Headless Rider has never been seen holding its own head that way. Perhaps it had one at some point, but when I witnessed it, there was no head under its arm, and after a thorough examination of all the Headless Rider videos uploaded online, I've never found any footage that falls under that description.

There are many pieces of evidence brought up to support the theory that the Headless Rider is a dullahan. One of them is a vague rumor that says the headless horse has the name "Shooter."

This is because a dullahan's horse-drawn carriage is called a Cóiste Bodhar, pronounced like "coshta bower." Apparently, we're to believe that the *shta* sound at the end of Cóiste was the basis for the name Shooter.

But that is honestly too ridiculous to be believed.

Why would an otherworldly creature like the Headless Rider come up with a nickname any third-grader could invent?

But the point I'm making is that rumors can spread even based on silly ideas like that one. And sometimes, an infinite curtain of rumors can conceal the truth behind it.

Perhaps it really is a dullahan, but the presence of so many unbelievable rumors is only making it harder to believe the truth.

While the Headless Rider shares many traits with the dullahan of legend, there is no explanation as to why a fairy from Ireland would be riding around Ikebukuro in Japan. I decided to keep that little tidbit in the back of my mind.

But what really draws my interest is the rider's connections to the Awakusu-kai mob group, which has an office in Ikebukuro, and the street gang known as the Dollars.

There's also a man wearing a bartender's uniform who is often seen active around the Headless Rider, which I find intriguing.

On top of that, there was a serial street slashing incident that shook Ikebukuro two years ago, known colloquially as the Night of the Ripper. When I heard rumors that the Headless Rider was involved in that, too, I could no longer contain myself.

From what I heard from Miss Niekawa, there was an information broker who knew about this sort of thing, but he had gone silent about a year and a half ago.

That timeline coincides with a bizarre incident in the Dollars, when the night sky over Ikebukuro was covered by shadow.

Could all these things be connected?

I feel as though these incidents, disparate dots on a map, might all actually form lines that lead to the Headless Rider at their center.

Over time, these doubts steadily transform further into certainty. I plan to continue gathering information and investigating what I find.

The Headless Rider is becoming an undeniable power within Ikebukuro.

A few years ago, there was a controversy over land speculators in Ikebukuro. One of them dressed up like a mock Headless Rider and roared all over the city, stirring up the residents. The idea was to turn the Headless Rider into a symbol of fear and danger, thus making the land less desirable and driving the price down—or perhaps they were working with a corrupt local politician who was hoping to get redevelopment rights.

The conclusion I am building to is that the Headless Rider is already considered an accepted fact of Ikebukuro by the people who live here.

Some of them may look positively upon this being, while others might revile it—but the fact of the matter is that most of the residents have accepted that the rider is simply something that can regularly be found here.

It is both an unidentified, mysterious monster and also a fact of regular life.

Could identifying this being bring about some change in the world? I entertain an illusion that it could.

But perhaps that is not an illusion.

Whether it can be made into an article or not is beside the point.

I want to discover the true nature of the Headless Rider to satisfy my own curiosity.

Notes:
Headless Rider is female?
Have on statement that she is called "Celty."
Connection to Dollars incident year and a half ago?
Connection to severed head thrown into public?
Head was stolen from police vehicle during attack, currently missing.
* During Dollars incident, Awakusu-kai and police station were shot at. Connection?!
Many witnesses on Kawagoe Highway.
Was able to make contact with influential intel provider.
Will meet tomorrow.
Results of meeting to follow.

♂♀

With that unfinished report, the rookie investigative writer Aya Tatsugami disappeared.

She had left the notebook computer with her text file on her desk in the office, still open. It was a quick list of information she typed in what must have been a hurry before leaving the building.

Text messages and calls to her went unanswered, and her family was equally without recourse to find her.

Who was this "influential intel provider" she intended to meet? Her coworkers and editors tried to find out, but they were unsuccessful.

They didn't even know how she was making contact with that provider—by phone, letter, or text message?

Naturally, she took her phone with her before disappearing, so there was no way to even peruse her call history without getting the police involved.

In the end, she simply vanished, leaving behind no hints for her publication's office. And in time, the story of the young writer searching for a lead on the Headless Rider created a new rumor.

A rumor that said she had learned the identity of the rider.

And that was why she had to be erased.

Had she been swallowed by the shadow of the Headless Rider or abducted by the Awakusu-kai?

So said the rumors, and just half a day after the missing person report had been filed, the information was on the Internet, and she, too, was absorbed into the urban legend surrounding the Headless Rider.

A newer, more macabre tail grew on the legend online. To wit: "Anyone who learns the identity of the Headless Rider loses their head and dies."

"The Headless Rider's been looking for its head for so long, and finally it gets the real thing."

"Snoop around after the Headless Rider for too long, and it will come after you."

"The Headless Rider sends messages to the phones of people who know too much about it."

"And the messages say, 'If you know that much, are you me? Are you my head?'"

"Then you look up, your head gets cut off, and the thing drags you into the shadows."

As the Japanese saying goes, a rumor lasts seventy-five days.

How many days do rumors of inhuman beings last? No one can say.

But there is one clear number we can point to.

Fifteen days have passed since Aya Tatsugami's disappearance.

She has not yet been confirmed alive.

CHAPTER 1 B
The Visitor

Ikebukuro—April

A boy from Akita came to Ikebukuro that day.

In this place, almost no one knew that he was feared as a monster in his hometown.

It was a completely new location for him, a doorway into an entirely new world. Ikebukuro was ready to welcome in a fresh face.

But whether this was indeed a new world for the boy or not would depend upon where fate would lead him, and whose orbit he would enter.

When he got off the bullet train and onto the Yamanote Line, he was shocked by the chaos of the Tokyo train experience. It was his first emotional reaction to the big city.

He had visited a few months ago to take the exams for his new school and then again last month to handle the final registration. But because he was staying with his relatives and got a car ride from the airport, he hadn't experienced the proper crush of mass transit here.

On this day, when he left his country home and traveled to the big city alone to reach his new place, the boy belatedly felt his first pangs of regret at choosing to attend high school in Tokyo.

People, people, people. Every direction he turned was packed, and back home, he hadn't experienced this kind of proximity to crowds, even at the most hectic festival events.

He was starting to feel dizzy in the crowd when a nearby sound distracted him: Adjacent passengers talking about rumors and gossip.

"Speakin' of Ikebukuro, is the Headless Rider still there?"

"I wonder. You don't see it in the news anymore."

"There was also that whole Dollars thing."

"Yeah, they were around the same time as the Headless Rider, right?"

He couldn't even move, it was so crowded, so the boy couldn't help but overhear their comments, although he had no idea what the people talking looked like. Based on their voices and way of speaking, however, he could guess that they were girls in high school or college.

Other sounds filled the train car, and the chaotic rhythm of it all made him feel queasy.

Eventually the train arrived at Ikebukuro Station, and the wave of humanity washed him right out of the car and down the stairs of the platform.

"Ikefukuro...," he muttered. The person from his apartment building had said to meet here. It was apparently a well-known spot.

He was three minutes ahead of the meeting time.

While he assumed he would be there in plenty of time, he was unable to find this Ikefukuro location, and by the time he had followed the station employees' answers to the right place, he was ten minutes late.

Ikefukuro, it turned out, was a statue of an owl. That clicked the answer into place—*fukuro* meant "owl."

But the space around the statue was absolutely stuffed with people. This was clearly a default meetup spot, and there was nowhere to stand because it was completely surrounded.

Fortunately, he soon heard a voice directed at him.

"Hi there, Yahiro. What's it been, about a month?"

He spun around and saw a man around age thirty wearing a suit.

Recognizing the man, the boy—Yahiro Mizuchi—quickly bowed in greeting.

"It's nice to see you again, Mr. Togusa."

"Hey, it's cool; you don't have to get all formal," said the man, walking closer. "I'll escort you home, then. Let's take a taxi."

He smiled, all prim and proper, and Yahiro bobbed his head again.

This man's name was Jirou Togusa.

He was a distant relative of Yahiro's father, who had taken the Mizuchi name when he married, and he was a young entrepreneur who managed several apartment buildings around Ikebukuro.

The apartment building adjacent to his home had an open unit, so he decided to lend it to Yahiro for lodging during his high school years. Yahiro was worried that it might be too much of an imposition, giving out a room for three whole years. But Jirou's older sister, who managed that building, reassured him, "Don't worry. That's a problematic apartment anyway, so we're not going to have any ordinary clients moving in there one way or another." That was an unwelcome bit of news.

"The truth is, I was going to have Saburo pick you up again, like he did when you came for your exam, but he's going to a Ruri Hijiribe concert today, so he was unavailable." Jirou chuckled ruefully in the back seat of the taxi, referring to his younger brother. "Saburo is crazy for her. If I recall correctly, I think his membership number in her fan club is in the single digits."

Saburo was the owner of a large van, and he was the one who gave Yahiro his rides when he visited for the school entrance exam. But for some reason, there were two of his friends in the back seat, a boy and girl, who spent the entire time talking about manga and anime, so Yahiro had very little memory of the guy who actually gave him the ride.

"Is Ruri Hijiribe popular in your generation, too?"

"Oh…yes. I'm a fan."

"Ah, good. It's good to be popular among the younger kids. I'm not big on idol culture or anything like that, but I'm very grateful to her in particular. My brother was a real ruffian, always getting into fights, but once he found an interest in her, it really shaped him into a proper person."

"…Fights?" Yahiro repeated warily.

Jirou laughed, unaware of what that might mean. "Yeah, I don't know much about that side of things, either—just that there were Blue somethings and the Dolls or whatever. He was involved in those groups. Now, he chums around with a couple of his friends. The leader of their little group is a guy named Kadota. It's strange; he's got this old-fashioned manliness about him. Works as a plasterer, so we've paid him to do some wall repairs on our buildings from time to time."

"Mr. Kadota, you say...?"

"That's right. Ikebukuro used to be overrun with street gangs a few years back. Then kids from Saitama would rush in and start big brawls. It was quite wild. But I hardly ever see those matching colors anymore. Even the kids with the yellow bandannas disappeared around last year or so."

Yahiro was more on the silent side, so Jirou was the one doing all the talking.

But that was a welcome development for Yahiro. It had been a very long time since anyone who wasn't his family spoke to him like a normal person like this.

He was curious. *How much did this guy hear about me from my family?*

Yahiro was aware of the kind of public figure he'd become in his hometown. That was why he had sought out this new horizon for himself.

He'd been dragged into fights he didn't want ever since he was a little boy.

If he had learned to just brush off bullies with a pleasant smile or two, he might have avoided the violence that ensued, but by the time he had grown enough to understand this, it was already too late for his reputation.

There were three things he hoped for in his new start in Ikebukuro.

First, he hoped he could lead a normal life in a distant place that had never heard of his infamy.

Second, if that was not possible, and he got wrapped up in fights anyway, he hoped that being in a place where superhuman inhabitants were a familiar part of life meant that he wouldn't be called a monster anymore.

That traveler he met at the inn, at least, agreed that he was human. That alone felt like a great salvation.

And the last thing that he hoped to have in Ikebukuro was a glimmer of optimism for his own future, something he'd largely given up on based on his last few years of life.

For now, though, he knew nothing about this place.

Everything he'd learned was from the Internet and magazines. He hadn't seen any of it for himself.

Yahiro steeled himself for the task ahead and observed the city outside the taxi through the window.

Jirou Togusa noticed him staring intently out the window and thought, *Ah, look at him watching so closely. He's probably got dreams of this new chapter of his life filling up his chest. He's a good kid. I hope Saburo learns something from him.*

He hadn't actually heard anything about Yahiro from the Mizuchis' side. He didn't know the first thing about the boy with him.

He had no idea how much terror the teenager inspired back in his hometown.

That was how a new boy came to Ikebukuro.

Just like all the other visitors, Ikebukuro welcomed him into its territory.

That was all that happened.

At least at this point in time.

♂♀

Raira Academy—several days later

Once the school ceremony was over and Yahiro went to his homeroom class, he was greeted by a very typical school event: new students introducing themselves to the rest of the class.

One by one, in seat number order, they stood in front of the blackboard, saying their names and providing a brief introduction of themselves.

The seating chart was determined by Japanese alphabetical order, which put Mizuchi close to the end.

Yahiro watched the event proceed with a pleasant mixture of excitement and nerves, soaking in the feeling of starting a new chapter in his life.

"I'm Kuon Kotonami. Heya."

Something in the class undeniably changed when one particular boy took his turn.

Yahiro had spotted him a few times before and after the entrance ceremony, but he didn't realize that they would be in the same class.

That's a wild hair color. It's green... Oh, right, this school lets you have dyed hair and piercings.

He decided this classmate must be in a band or something like that. Or maybe it was normal fashion for Tokyo—he'd never seen it back home.

But then Yahiro noticed the other people in class seemed equally fascinated and thought better of this assumption.

Well, based on the way he talks, he doesn't seem like a total barbarian...I think.

He tried to remember the various people who had tangled with him back home, but the memories were vague. To Yahiro, those delinquents were not so much people as beings that came threatening unfair violence—objects of fear.

And in the end, he was always the one who got called a monster.

That wasn't fair. He was the one who wanted to call *them* monsters. They were the ones threatening strangers with violence for no reason at all—wasn't that enough to warrant the label?

Thinking about his past was making Yahiro feel depressed. He decided he should focus on the introductions again to put that feeling out of his mind.

But the green-haired boy had left such an impact on Yahiro that he didn't really pay that much attention until a very pretty girl took her turn.

"I'm Himeka Tatsugami. It's nice to meet you," she said. She had a slender figure, black hair, and did not wear much makeup.

She had a quiet demeanor but was not bashful or intimidated. The girl was simply self-assured and pure of heart, and her voice made Yahiro feel calm just from listening to it.

Huh. I thought that all the girls in Tokyo were, like, smearing shoe polish all over their faces. I guess not. What was that trend called again? Ganguro?

What kind of research on Tokyo had Yahiro done, either in magazines or websites, before he came here? For some reason, he was envisioning the metropolitan teen trends from over a decade before, so the fact that most of the girls in class weren't sporting tans and flashy makeup was stunning to him.

While he silently grappled with this culture shock, the class introductions continued running down the list—until at last, it was his turn.

*   *   *

"Uh…I'm Yahiro Mizuchi. I came from Akita. It's nice to meet you."

There we go. I didn't let any funky Akita dialect into my introduction… right?

Yahiro's father was born in Tokyo, and many of the tourists at the inn came from here, too. He'd had enough books and DVDs around the house and enough exposure to the standard Tokyo dialect that it wasn't hard for him to do it, too.

In fact, because he rarely spoke at school and had no friends, it was harder for him to speak the particular dialect of his home region.

But while he couldn't actually speak in the very strong accent his grandmother and mother used, he could understand it. And because his grandmother needed to be able to understand standard Japanese to run the inn, there was never any trouble communicating around the house.

Still, he'd been worried that he might not be able to adequately speak this dialect of Japanese. Judging by the reactions of the class, it seemed he did fine.

Looking from the front of the class over the rows of seats, he was keenly aware that all their eyes were concentrated on him. But those eyes were full of only curiosity—no fear or disgust or hatred.

And the students who had no interest in him didn't bother to meet his gaze at all.

Now that he was here, the boy felt certain of one thing: This was a fresh environment for him, a place where his reputation could start over from scratch.

He stood there, savoring a feeling that only he could understand, until there was some light questioning from the class, as they'd done with the others. Yahiro assumed no one would have any questions for him, and he'd end up returning to his seat without needing to answer anything.

But one of the girls latched onto the keyword *Akita* and asked him a question without raising her hand first.

"Why did you come here from Akita? It's not like this school is a university feeder or anything."

That was a perfectly reasonable question, but he wasn't sure how to respond.

Why had he come to Ikebukuro?

It wasn't because he was fascinated by the big city and wanted to be in it.

He didn't have family problems that forced him to move.

That was when he came to a realization.

If Raira Academy was a famous school along the university track, that would be one thing. But the vast majority of students here were local or from neighboring prefectures. The idea that someone would move here from Akita, all the way in northeast Japan, made Yahiro a strange and curious phenomenon to them.

But Yahiro was not the kind of person built to come up with convincing lies on the spot. And he didn't think that lying about this would be worth it.

But on the other hand…I probably shouldn't mention the fighting. I think.

He'd spent a lonely childhood being shunned by others who were frightened of him, so Yahiro didn't quite have the social skills to maneuver through this kind of awkward situation.

But he thought hard and fast, and he arrived at an answer that wasn't a lie but also concealed a major part of his story.

"Um…"

If only it hadn't sounded like a bit of a joke to his classmates.

"…I came here to see the Headless Rider."

They chuckled and giggled, but that reaction only confused him.

…???

Did I say something funny?

It wasn't mocking laughter, more like polite chuckles for the new student telling a joke. There was no social faux pas happening.

But Yahiro couldn't avoid a sudden panic at the idea that perhaps the Headless Rider was never real. What was he supposed to do then?

"I guess that makes sense. There's no Headless Rider in Akita!"

"I see the rider all the time."

"But not much lately, right?" said a group of girls to Yahiro's relief.

Oh, good. So the Headless Rider is real.

A quick survey of the room brought something to his attention, however.

Two of the people who had not been paying attention during Yahiro's introduction were now watching him with keen interest.

…?

One was the green-haired boy named Kuon Kotonami.

The other was the pretty girl named Himeka Tatsugami.

Kuon was smiling, but it was a different kind of smile from the others, it seemed to Yahiro.

His eyes were gleaming the way a child's do when he sees a cool toy.

While that was worrisome, Yahiro was more worried about Himeka's gaze.

There was no real expression on her face—but it *especially* was not a smile.

Her eyes were only sharp and cold, staring at him intently—but in his current state, he was unable to come up with anything to say to her.

♂♀

After school

His first day of school successfully finished, Yahiro began to gather his belongings.

The students around him had already gotten ready to leave, and they took off, chatting with their friends and acquaintances from middle school.

Naturally, he did not know anyone from middle school here. And if he did, they would be anything but friends. None of them would want to walk home from school with him, that much was certain.

Friends... I've never had friends. He sighed, thinking, *If I do make one, they'll probably freak out if they find out about my past. If it's going to end in misery and rejection no matter what, maybe it'll be easier not to make friends at all.*

Yahiro put his papers away, slung his bag over his shoulder, and stood up. Then he crossed over to the window to look outside.

The sight of Ikebukuro was dramatically different from what he was used to back home. He felt a strange kind of elation come over him.

What is this feeling? I guess it's...excitement? I don't think I've ever felt this emotion before.

There was a throbbing pulse deep in his gut that traveled upward, forcing a grin to break out over his face. Assuming that the classroom would be empty by now, he spun around on his heel...

                        *   *   *

...and came face-to-face with a girl.

He flinched, and then he looked at her again.

It was a face he couldn't forget.

Himeka Tatsugami was staring at him the same way she had earlier.

"...Is something funny?" she asked, rubbing her cheek.

Yahiro came back to his senses with a start. He realized that he was still grinning from ear to ear.

"Er, no, nothing. I was just looking at the city and smiling."

"...Is there something funny about it?"

"No, not really."

"Uh-huh...," murmured Himeka. She looked over her shoulder at the sight out the window.

Yahiro had no idea what he should do in this situation, so he froze in place.

The classroom was completely empty except for the two of them.

Wasn't she going to leave school with her local friends?

When she'd had her fill of looking out the window, she turned back to Yahiro and said, "You're strange."

"Uh...I am?"

What should I do? Maybe I've actually said something really rude to her.

When she called him "strange," he didn't sense that it was said with hostility or mockery. But Yahiro had so little positive human interaction in his life, he couldn't eliminate the nagging feeling that he had made some mistake along the way.

The girl's face was still an emotionless mask. "Hey."

"Wh-what?"

"Was that a joke earlier? Or were you serious?"

"Earlier?"

What should I do? Maybe I did do something wrong.

He thought back on all the things he'd done today, but before he could figure it out, she elaborated, "When you said you wanted to see the Headless Rider, during your introduction."

"Huh?" Yahiro nervously said with a pause. Then he recalled what he'd done. "Ohhh, that..."

"Well? Was it a joke?"

"…Did everyone think that was a joke?"

"Huh?" Now it was Himeka's turn to be confused. "I mean, I assume that's why they laughed."

"Oh, okay… I get it now."

So they thought I was joking. That's why they were laughing. But… why did they think it was a joke? Is wanting to see the Headless Rider such a strange reason for coming here?

To the people of Ikebukuro, the Headless Rider was no longer a rare or novel thing. So they assumed that no one would actually choose to spend three whole years of their life in school here to see something so ordinary. They figured it had to be a joke.

They didn't realize that to Yahiro, this was more than just three years—it was something that had the potential to change the course of his entire life.

This girl couldn't possibly know that, either.

"Well, thanks for telling me," he said. "That answers my question."

She looked slightly befuddled at that. She didn't know why he would be thanking her. But her overall expression did not break. Instead, she asked, "Then…you're serious?"

"Well, it's one of my reasons."

"…Oh," Himeka murmured. Then she stated flatly, "I don't think you should."

"Huh?"

"Don't dig too deeply into the Headless Rider."

"Why not?" His tone was frank.

But Himeka only shook her head. "I can't tell you."

"Huh?"

"The point is, I've given you a warning."

Then she turned on her heel and started marching away.

"Wait!"

An ordinary boy might have been rooted to the spot, helplessly watching her go—but Yahiro's reflexes, honed by years of fighting, kicked in automatically as she left.

Without a moment's hesitation, he reached out, grabbed the back of her collar, and forcefully yanked her backward.

"Huh…*llgh*…"

The pressure on her throat stopped her breathing as he dragged her back.

"...!"

She flopped and kicked her legs, until Yahiro realized what he was doing and hastily let go.

"What?! I-I'm sorry! I didn't mean to..."

Once her coughing subsided, Himeka continued breathing heavily and fixed Yahiro with a stare.

"...I wasn't expecting you to hold me back to the point of strangulation," she said, although there was no hatred there, only pure shock.

But for some reason, either from her innate nature or perhaps some inability on her part to express herself, it was simply impossible to read the look on her face.

"I'm really sorry. Are you all right?"

"Yes, I'm fine now."

"Sorry...I just got really scared."

"...Scared?" she repeated.

Yahiro explained, "Yeah. See, I'm more cowardly than the average person... And you said something that worried me and claimed you couldn't explain it...so I got really scared all of a sudden. Er, not that any of this excuses what I did. I'm sorry."

He bowed deeply to show his contrition. Himeka exhaled deeply and said, "So you're cowardly...but you want to see the Headless Rider?"

"Yeah. *Because* I'm cowardly."

"?"

"I've been through a lot."

That didn't seem to clear things up for Himeka, who had no response. But when she realized he wasn't going to elaborate on it, she said, "You really are strange."

"You think so?"

"Why don't we make a trade, then?"

"A trade?" Yahiro repeated. It was his turn to be confused.

"If you tell me why you want to see the Headless Rider, I'll tell you why I think you should stay away," she said. It was still blunt, but her demeanor seemed a bit more positive than before.

"Well..."

"It can be tomorrow, though. It's not like you're going to walk around the city looking for the Headless Rider today, right?"

"W-well, it's only my first day here," he admitted.

She nodded slowly. "Then I guess you'll be fine."

Himeka straightened out her collar, then started walking away. When she reached the door of the classroom, she paused and turned back to him again.

"I'm sorry."

"Huh?"

He didn't understand why she would be apologizing.

She went on. "What I said earlier... I didn't mean to frighten you. It really was just a warning."

All Yahiro could do was watch as she left. This time, he did not pull her back.

♂♀

Outside the school gate

"Man, I really should have apologized about grabbing her collar one more time for good measure," Yahiro lamented, plodding off the school grounds and stewing in self-loathing.

As he passed through the gate, a boy called out to him.

"Hey! How ya doin', Yahiro?"

It sounded like someone greeting a friend he'd known for years. But in fact, it was a boy he'd just met today at the class introductions—someone whose face only needed one glance to recognize.

"Uhhh...Kotomine, was it?"

"What? No, no! It's Kotonami! Ko-to-na-mi! But you can call me Kuon. It's easier to remember, right? Since I already jumped ahead to calling you Yahiro, that makes us even!" Kuon Kotonami chuckled, and his green-dyed hair waved in the wind.

Much like with Himeka minutes earlier, Yahiro was initially confused as to why his classmate had singled him out for intimate conversation.

Um...did I do something to him?

But in the meantime, Kuon rattled him with a barrage of machine-gun chatter.

"I was waiting for you to come out, but you never did. Thought maybe you were checking out the school or something. I probably should have done that, too, come to think of it. Tomorrow's when all the school clubs get to start recruiting new students, so it'll be harder to take a nice easy tour. Did you already decide what club or committee you wanna join? I'd recommend the library committee. What do you think? Personally, I think they're all annoying, so I'm not gonna bother joining anything."

"...Oh. Thanks for telling me," Yahiro replied, unsure of what else to say.

Kuon slapped him on the back and continued talking. "I just had a feeling when you made your introduction! I knew I would be good friends with you, Yahiro! We have the same motive for coming here!"

"Huh?" Yahiro gaped.

Kuon beamed at him. "You doing anything after this? Got any plans?"

"Nothing until I go back to where I'm staying."

"Uh-huh. Got a curfew, then? Well, common sense says you should be fine until eight o'clock, right?"

"Uh. I guess," Yahiro murmured.

Kuon clapped his hands. "Then it's settled! Let's go!"

"Go where?"

"Into Ikebukuro. My guess is probably around West Gate Park."

"To do what?" Yahiro asked. He assumed it was probably to try to pick up girls or something.

What should I say? I've never done anything like that. I don't want to be the guy who becomes a big bummer to his classmate on the first day of school... I already got myself in enough trouble by choking Tatsugami...

Despite Yahiro's oddly misplaced worries, Kuon's answer was quite straightforward.

"What else would we do? Go searching."

"For what?"

"For *what*?" Kuon repeated. He shrugged, grinned, and gave an enthusiastic thumbs-up to the sky. "Let's go and find that Headless Rider ourselves!"

INTERMISSION
Online Rumors (1)

On the Ikebukuro information site IkeNew! Version I.KEBU.KUR.O

```
Popular Post: [The Urban Legend Is Over]
Haven't seen the Headless Rider around, huh
```

"Where did the Headless Rider go?" (Rehosted from *Tokyo Warrior* online site)

When people mention the urban legend that once freely strolled around Ikebukuro, they are referring, of course, to the Headless Rider. But in the last six months, eyewitness reports of the rider have fallen off a cliff.

The Headless Rider became a national sensation when it was clearly filmed in the midst of a Daioh TV live report accompanying a police operation. But what's underappreciated by the public at large is that sightings of the rider in Tokyo have been reported for over twenty years.

The president of a show business production company placed a huge bounty on it, leading to the phenomenon of "Headless Rider Hunts," but even after they died down, it never seemed bothered. Onward went the darkened night rides.

The Headless Rider straddles a silent motorcycle that transforms into a headless horse and swings a pitch-black scythe. It's the kind of sight that sears itself into the psyche as vividly as any traumatic experience, but when it happened on the main roads all the time, there was no end of the sightings.

Half a year ago, however, uploads of Headless Rider footage to video sites simply stopped. Run a search on various social media networks for the Headless Rider, and all you'll find are people talking about how they *haven't* seen the ghostly figure anymore.

Has the Headless Rider vanished from Ikebukuro for good?

The Ikebukuro-based writer Shinichi Tsukumoya wrote on his blog, "The Headless Rider is simply tired of creating legends. After it has rested, it will surely return to its familiar haunt."

—(The rest of this article can be read at the original link)

Comment from IkeNew! *Administrator*

Know that this rider's been seen around for over twenty years, I did not.

If they started riding around age twenty, over forty now, that would make them.

Realized that it's embarrassing to be a forty-year-old cosplaying as a spooky ghost and driving around the city, perhaps they have?

By that age, they should be more down-to-earth and normal, you would expect.

And yes, that means I'm talking to all you forty-somethings reading this who are into cartoons for children, too.

Admin: Rira Tailtooth Zaiya

♂♀

A selection of representative twits from the social network Twittia

Haven't seen the Headless Rider in a while.

→ It's gone, huh? One-hit wonder. One and done.

→ No way. It was around when I was a kid.

→I mean, it was around since my dad was in school.

→How old is the Headless Rider anyway?

Speaking of the Headless Rider, you remember that crazy thing two years back? Where the sky got all dark, and it was still black in the morning hours. I wonder if that was the Headless Rider's shadow.

→Oh yeah, yeah! I wonder what that was all about.

→Didn't they say it was dust storms?

→There is no damn way that was a dust storm. I mean, things were crazy that night. Biker gangs all over the damn place. Wasn't there a shooting, too?

→Oh yeah, yeah. Didn't some teenager catch a stray bullet from the bikers and die?

→I thought he survived.

→Yeah, it wasn't fatal.

→I wasn't talking about that, I was thinking of the Awakusu-kai and police station getting shot up.

I wonder if we'll ever get to see the Headless Rider again.

→I'll manage. It's freaky when you're in a car and it just breezes past you.

→Actually, I'm amazed that never caused any big traffic accidents. No headlights!

→The Headless Rider might not care, but we get freaked out.

→Traffic cops need all the help they can get.

I finally did it. I might get to meet the Headless Rider.

Tomorrow I'm going to get to talk to someone who knows the legendary Headless Rider! I can't wait!

→How did this go?

→You didn't tweet an update. But you tweeted every single day before that.

→It's like a horror movie.

→Maybe the rider made them disappear lol

  →That's not funny. They really did disappear.

   →What?! Holy crap! I'm sorry.

→Everyone's clearly worried, so you should probably tweet again if you're all right.

CHAPTER 2

CHAPTER 2 A
The Missing

The Awakusu-kai of the Medei-gumi Syndicate was a gathering of *professional gentlemen* claiming territory all over Ikebukuro. You know the kind.

Led by a man named Dougen Awakusu, they were a powerful faction within the Medei-gumi, and their name prompted fear and caution among not only the local police but also major businesses and the media.

One of their lieutenants, a man named Shiki, was summoned to the Awakusu office early in the morning.

Unsure what this was about, Shiki arrived at the office feeling wary—and when he reported in, he caught a stray bullet from a direction he would never have expected.

"Missing, you say?"

Shiki was sitting across an elegant wooden desk from a man seated in a leather-bound chair—the future heir to the Awakusu-kai, Mikiya Awakusu.

"That's right," said Mikiya. "It's been happening in our business territory, mostly among young folks."

Mikiya was the boss's second son and supposedly the first in line to succeed, but some in the organization did not think highly of him. He had to be vigilant and avoid vulnerability.

In recent years, it was becoming less and less common for organized crime to pass down leadership directly to their children. Mikiya's brother, the eldest, had chosen an ordinary life for himself. So it was known that Mikiya was dedicated to this line of work.

When people murmured that he was spoiled by his father's favor, he crushed them. The current rivalry playing out was between him and another lieutenant named Aozaki.

"From kids around fifteen to magazine writers in their twenties," he said, making a bitter face.

It took several seconds of careful contemplation before Shiki replied, "It's the first I've heard. How many are we talking about?"

"I don't know for certain, but I'm aware of fifteen cases within the past month."

"..."

Shiki mulled this over.

He must be getting this information from a mole within the police. In that case, I should assume the number is accurate. And fifteen people disappearing certainly sounds like a lot...

But then he reconsidered.

The number of missing people recorded in the system varied from year to year. A general annual number for the entire nation of Japan was about eighty thousand. In a busy year, it could easily top a hundred thousand. Fifteen was not a lot in the big scheme of things.

"Considering the population of Tokyo and the number of runaways and such, it's not really that surprising, is it? Doesn't seem worth raising a fuss about."

Of course, not every missing person simply vanishes off the face of the earth, and the majority of cases are solved after the missing person's report is filed.

"I mean, if these are kids, we could be talking about mere runaways... Er, begging your pardon, sir. Wasn't referring to Miss Akane," Shiki said, bobbing his head.

Mikiya had a daughter by the name of Akane Awakusu. She had run away from home for several days two years ago as an elementary school student.

"No, it's fine. At first, I thought it was kids running away, too, like my daughter. But..."

"What is it? You don't think our company's involved, do you?"

"That's exactly it. I mean, I want to believe we're not, but from what I know, the police are suspecting our involvement with the string."

"Why would they?"

The Awakusu-kai was a criminal organization. *Disappearing people* was part of the business.

But as far as Shiki knew, they weren't in the habit of erasing ordinary citizens from the streets. If the magazine writer had gotten hold of some juicy nugget of info and tried their hand at blackmail, that would be one thing, but nobody had any reason to get rid of teenagers in school.

Maybe if the Awakusu-kai were dealing drugs and the kids were bottom-rung sellers—but that was exactly the problem. The Awakusu-kai didn't sell drugs as part of their business. Part of that was because the boss hated drugs, and part of it was that the powerful lieutenant Akabayashi *especially* hated drugs. Nobody in the group wanted to stick their hand in that fire.

On the other hand, because they weren't relying on the easy income of drugs, the Awakusu-kai had to lean more heavily on their local business, which made it tricky to avoid angering the populace of the city.

So if there were rumors that the Awakusu-kai was involved in people going missing, that did not bode well for the group.

Understanding at last why Mikiya was grimacing, Shiki gave the problem his renewed attention. The leather chair creaked as Mikiya readjusted his position. He asked Shiki, "Do you know about the Headless Rider?"

"..."

"You do, don't you? The courier that you and Akabayashi hire from time to time."

"Well, yes. But the rider's been out of the business lately," Shiki admitted.

Mikiya continued, "I understand that Akane knows the rider as well. I've heard her mention that."

"Yes, the Headless Rider helped us when the young mistress ran away from home."

"I'm going to be direct with you. Who is the Headless Rider?" Mikiya demanded, his eyes narrowing. "I assume it's not *truly* headless, of course."

"There's no head, sir."

"...What?"

"It's difficult to believe, but it's the truth," Shiki stated.

Mikiya smacked the desk. "This is no time for bullshit, man!"

Most people would have shriveled up in the face of his anger, but Shiki remained cool. Respectfully, he replied, "Sir, you of all people should know that I am not the type to speak bullshit at moments like this."

"..."

Mikiya clammed up. He had a point; Akabayashi might shrug off a question like that with a joke, but Shiki was not such a man, and Mikiya knew it.

That still didn't make it any easier for him to accept his answer.

"But...wait. Wait a minute. If it has no head...then you're saying it's literally a headless rider."

"Yes. The Headless Rider is a headless rider. I understand why you'd doubt it, but I can introduce you sometime. Mr. Dougen is already aware of this."

"...Dad knows?"

Now that he'd brought the name of the company president into it, there was no way Mikiya could possibly accuse him of lying. Not a single person in the Awakusu-kai would swear on Dougen's name and tell a falsehood.

Mikiya didn't quite accept the answer, but he realized he wasn't going to win further arguments. Somewhat awkwardly, he tried to move on.

"...Well, we can discuss that later. I don't care if the Headless Rider is real or just a stage magician. The real issue is that it might be involved in these disappearances."

"...Really?"

"Yes. From what I understand...all the people who vanished were passionate fans of the Headless Rider."

"Uh...fans?" Shiki repeated, taken aback by that word.

"That's right. People who had an interest in the Headless Rider and were trying to track it down. From what I understand, these kids with big dreams have taken to worshipping it like some kind of pop singer... And the writer who vanished was working on some kind of scoop."

"But people like that have been around for years. Why now...?"

"That's what I want to know. I know there have been freelance journalists looking into the Headless Rider's story, but this person's the first one to actually disappear. The problem is, this story's reached the Internet."

"Ah, I see. And so they're also talking about connections between us and the Headless Rider, I assume," Shiki added.

Mikiya exhaled. He was clearly quite upset about all this, a vulnerable position for a major yakuza lieutenant to be in, but it was a sign of how much he trusted Shiki to let him witness it.

He put his hands on the desk, fingers steepled, and looked Shiki in the eyes. "One of the people who went missing is a student at Akane's new middle school."

"..."

"I suppose Akane must be feeling responsible for what happened when she ran away. Apparently, when she heard about the rumors that the rider did it, she said, 'The Headless Rider wouldn't do that,' and now she's gone off searching on her own."

"Whether the Headless Rider is actually involved or not, that's probably something you'd want to stop," Shiki admitted. If the rider he knew was responsible for the disappearances, Akane was obviously in danger. Even though she would know Akane by appearance and position, if she was vanishing people left and right, something *wrong* was going on.

And if the Headless Rider wasn't at fault, that meant some mystery abductors were likely to catch rumor of Akane and put her through the same thing they'd done to the others.

"I scolded her, of course. But you know what my daughter is like."

"That's true. She might obey you in person, but she'd cook up some plan in secret."

"I can only imagine where she gets it..."

"..."

Brother Mikiya was like that when he was younger, too, thought

Shiki, remembering how Mikiya had spurned Dougen Awakusu's warnings and gotten into trouble in his youth. He chose not to mention that now. He was not clever enough to get away with teasing his superiors in person.

Mikiya moved on. "Anyway, if you can get in touch with the Headless Rider, that would make things easy. Bring this guy here right now... No, wait. Not to the office or any of our other spots. Pick out someplace appropriate and see if you can get any information direct from the source."

"...'Right now' may not be possible, sir."

"What do you mean?" Mikiya asked.

Shiki shook his head. "The courier's stepped back from the business...and gone on vacation with that black market doctor."

"Vacation?" repeated Mikiya, confused. Shiki followed up with an explanation.

"Forget the last month. The Headless Rider hasn't been around in the past half a year."

CHAPTER 2 B
The Instigator

Ikebukuro—Rakuei Gym, night

Of all the martial arts gyms to be found in Ikebukuro, Rakuei Gym was one of the biggest.

On paper, the German MMA world champion, Traugott Geissendorfer, was a member, and for that reason, the gym's name was known worldwide.

It was a mixed martial arts gym for the most part, but it had different floors for specific disciplines like karate and boxing. You could even take weapon lessons with swords, spears, and staffs.

Their members varied from serious disciples to housewives looking for an effective weight loss method. If you took out the particular kind of tension that all fighting gyms have, it was an eccentric place where people of all kinds could be found. In that sense, it was much like the city itself.

"Wow, I wouldn't have guessed that you go here, too, Kuon! I'm a bit shocked, actually," said Mairu, who was dressed in her fighting *dogi*.

Kuon, still in his school uniform by contrast, scratched his head awkwardly. "Well…I went to the Takadanobaba location up through middle school…but now this location is easier to stop by on the way home from school."

"Got it, got it. Well, it's wild to think that Aocchi introduced you to me during spring vacation, and we're already running into each other here."

"I'm just as shocked as you."

At the start of every school year, it wasn't particularly rare to find fellow students having conversations like these—if perhaps not this precise circumstance.

But no sooner had the mood settled than Mairu broke it down by glancing behind Kuon. "So who's this boy?"

"Oh…sorry. Um, hello," said another boy wearing the same school uniform, bowing and looking around nervously. It was Yahiro. "I'm Kuon's classmate. My name is Yahiro Mizuchi."

"Ohhh. So you're another one of my underclassmen, then! Hi there."

"Thank you. It's nice to meet you."

Mairu gave the nervous new boy a close examination. She was wearing special athletic glasses at the moment, although she took them off when performing fiercer activity like sparring and competition.

"Hmm—hmm—hmm. No dyed hair, no piercings. I don't smell cigarette smoke or paint thinner. That's great! Unlike Kuon, you seem like a model student."

"Uh…th-thank you?" Yahiro replied, unsure why he was being assessed like this.

But Kuon, cheek twitching, rounded on the older girl in protest. "Hey, uh, I don't smoke or huff thinner, either…"

"That's true. Although if you're hanging out with Aocchi, you're probably up to much worse."

"H-hey, that's not fair!" complained Kuon, as Mairu cackled.

Yahiro stared at the two opposites in wonder. She turned to him and asked, "So are you looking to join?"

"Um, I'm just observing for today…"

Then Kuon interjected, "That's right, he's a stick-in-the-mud, Mairu!" and jabbed Yahiro with his elbow. "We were supposed to be going to look for the Headless Rider together, but Yahiro's no fun!"

♂♀

Outside school

One hour earlier…

"Let's go and find that Headless Rider ourselves!" Kuon said, all momentum and excitement.

But Yahiro quickly replied, "No, I'll pass for today."

"Wha—? Why?! You're not doing anything!"

"Yes. I'm fine doing something else...but I'm not thinking of looking for the Headless Rider until at least tomorrow. That's the one thing I'm not ready for today," Yahiro said. His voice was gentle but firm.

Kuon was flustered. "Why is today not the right day for the Headless Rider?! What does that mean?!"

"..."

Yahiro considered his answer. *What should I tell him? I was going to follow Tatsugami's advice and at least wait until tomorrow...*

But mentioning that felt like it would be revealing a secret, and he wasn't sure if it would be proper. She didn't swear him to secrecy or anything like that, but he had the sense that it wasn't the kind of conversation meant to be repeated to others.

So he told Kuon, "Sorry, the reason's a secret. I couldn't even tell a friend."

"What? Is it that important?!"

"I don't know if *important* is the right word..."

The sight of Yahiro seriously uncertain of how to explain it gave Kuon a strange sensation of culture shock. Beads of sweat broke out on his forehead. "You really are weird..."

"Huh?! I...I am?"

Uh-oh. Where did I go wrong?

Yahiro was not the most adept at judging the proper emotional distance of a friend, so he adopted what he thought was a polite smile—but not being used to smiling, it just looked like an awkward grimace.

Kuon wasn't quite sure how to respond to this, either. He sighed. "Well, I guess we don't have to do it *today*. Maybe I'll go visit the dojo instead."

"Dojo?"

"Yeah, it's called Rakuei Gym. I've been going to the dojo in Takadanobaba, but now my high school's over here, right? So I'm going to visit the main location in Ikebukuro."

"Dojo... Like, for martial arts? What do you do there?" asked Yahiro, suddenly eager and interested.

Kuon wasn't sure what to make of that, but he kept up a friendly smile nevertheless. "Oh, all kinds of stuff. I'm learning self-defense. But you can do anything—mixed martial arts, karate, boxing, kendo, you name it."

Yahiro's eyes widened a bit. He considered this for a moment.

"Can I ask you some more questions about that?"

♂♀

And that was how Yahiro came to be at Rakuei Gym to observe the offerings there.

"I can't believe it. He moved here to Ikebukuro, and he's going to be all passive and hesitant about checking out the Headless Rider? It's unthinkable. You're just wasting your time." Kuon grumbled, clearly not over their change of plans.

"Huh? You guys are interested in the Headless Rider?" asked Mairu.

"Well, yeah. I was definitely curious to check this whole thing out. But Yahiro is, like, obsessed. He says he came to Tokyo from Akita—just to see the Headless Rider. That's crazy, right?"

"Wow, all the way from Akita?! That's some dedication! Very cool," exclaimed Mairu, her eyes sparkling.

Yahiro's wandered aimlessly. "Er, well...I guess the Headless Rider...isn't my *only* reason..."

"What? What's that? What are you after? Is it my body?! But you can't! Every inch of my body belongs to Kuru and Yuuhei! It's been preordered! Already sold out!"

"I'm sorry. I...don't know what you mean...," stammered Yahiro.

Kuon muttered into his ear, "I've only known her for a little while, but I know you can ignore when she's being annoying like this. Plus, I don't think it's worth coming all the way from Akita for *her* body. Her sister, on the other hand—"

"*I can hear you!*" Mairu grunted, swiftly spinning behind Kuon's back and grinding his temples with her fists.

"Aaaaah! H-hey, isn't this the kind of thing little kids do?! It's like slapping hands or flicking foreheads! I've never actually seen someone do this in real liii— Aaaaaow!"

"Well, I'm certainly not going to be telling any naughty underclassmen like you any tidbits I know about the Headless Rider!"

Tidbits about the Headless Rider. Yahiro and Kuon pounced upon the offhand mention.

"Huh?"

"Hey, Mairu, could you please tell me how much you know?"

She grinned and hissed laughter through her teeth. "Oh, lots. I've met the rider several times. Kuru even got the Headless Rider as a bodyguard once."

"Bodyguard?" Yahiro said. That word didn't seem to have any relation to the urban legend he was familiar with.

"Yep. I mean, our brother was friends with the Headless Rider."

"Friends…?" Yahiro was even more confused than before.

Kuon gave her a piercing look. "Now there you go again, making up stuff to tease younger people who don't know better."

"What's that look for? You don't believe me? I'm not joking, and I'm not some habitual liar. You can ask Kuru or Aocchi for the truth."

"Ask Kuronuma?" Kuon repeated, frowning.

Yahiro looked from Mairu to Kuon with confusion. "Who's that?"

"Hmm…? Oh, he's an older kid who helped me out when I was in middle school," Kuon explained vaguely.

Mairu added, "He's the boss of a big scary group of bad boys, so be careful of him, okay?"

"Hey, read the room! I was trying to avoid details!"

"I did read the room. And then I ignored it, so don't worry!"

"Ugh, you're the worst!" Kuon lamented. But he realized the cat was out of the bag, so he followed up with, "First of all, Mairu is completely wrong that he's the leader of some army of thugs. There are a few intimidating people in the group—that's all. You know, guys who are quick to jump into a fight…"

Then he realized that he was not exactly reassuring his audience and tried to change the subject. "A-anyway! If your brother is supposed to be friends with the Headless Rider, then that makes things super-easy! Go ahead—call him up right now! Call, call, call, on that celly-cell-cell!" he chanted, slapping the gym's pillar with his palm.

Mairu just laughed. "Ha-ha-ha-ha, I can't."

"Why not? It's not fair! You can't bring that up and then say you won't!" Kuon protested.

But her expression didn't ease the tiniest bit as she admitted, "I can't because my brother's been missing for *over a year.*"

It was a bombshell.

"…"

"…"

The two boys in uniform shared a look but no words.

Mairu seemed unfazed by their shock, however. She went on, "Oh, it's fine; don't worry about it. He's vanished a bunch of times before—this one just happens to be longer than usual."

That was a bit of a relief to Yahiro. "Oh…I see."

But that feeling did not last long. She said, "Plus, if at worst he happens to be at the bottom of Tokyo Bay, then that's a fitting end for my brother. Especially if you assume he probably wanted it that way, y'know?"

"…"

Yahiro was once again intimidated into silence. This time it was Kuon who spoke up.

"Uh…that sounds really worrying, though… If one of the Headless Rider's acquaintances vanished, that's just like what's been…"

Before he could finish his sentence, a different voice joined the conversation.

"You're wrong."

"?"

"The Headless Rider wouldn't do that."

The trio turned toward the voice and saw a girl a whole head shorter than Yahiro, wearing a white cotton vest and white hakama, a kind of traditional pleated trousers tied high around the stomach. In her hand was an octagonal pole carved from evergreen oak, indicating that she was attending the gym to learn polearm combat.

Mairu recognized the girl at once. "Oh, it's Akane. Heya!"

"It's nice to see you, Miss Orihara," said Akane, bowing politely.

Kuon asked, "Uh, who are you?"

"…I am Akane Awakusu, a pupil of Rakuei-Style Jodo," she said, referring to a form of combat using short staffs. Like with Mairu, she bowed very politely to the boys.

"Oh, uh, I'm only here to observe. I'm Yahiro Mizuchi."

"Kuon Kotonami. Nice to meet you, young lady."

"It's a pleasure," Akane said, taking their first introductions very seriously. Then she insisted, "The Headless Rider is not going to kidnap you."

They had no idea when she started listening in. But at the very least, it seemed that she had something to say about Kuon's suggestion that Mairu's brother's disappearance was related to the Headless Rider.

Yahiro, of course, had no way of knowing why she felt that way, so he could add nothing to the discussion. He just listened closely.

"Everyone has the wrong idea. The Headless Rider isn't some scary monster like everyone online says…," Akane noted mournfully.

Yahiro felt something in his heart twinge. *Huh? What…is this feeling…?*

It didn't take long for him to recognize the strange sensation rising within his chest.

The people back home who called him a monster.

The people who looked at the Headless Rider the same way.

Did that mean he was hoping to look at the Headless Rider just like that, too?

Was he here to see the Headless Rider so that he could prove to himself that he was normal? Was that not the height of arrogance?

This sudden epiphany threw Yahiro into a deep and sudden malaise.

…Have I been acting incredibly rude toward the Headless Rider…? Then I guess that makes me no better than an inhuman monster…

Completely oblivious to his classmate's sudden funk, Kuon asked, "Akane, right? Are you saying you know the Headless Rider, Akane?"

"…"

She did not answer his question. If anything, she seemed wary of him.

That was a natural reaction to his shocking green hair and piercings, but there seemed to be more to her reaction, too, swirling beneath the surface.

"Hey, don't get all freaked out! This is all just, uh— You know how frogs in the jungle have some crazy colors sometimes? Like poison dart frogs. It's just as harmless as that."

"Those are lethally poisonous," Mairu noted.

"It literally says poison in the name…," Yahiro added.

Kuon ignored their comments and tried to win over Akane with friendliness. "Plus, none of us said we think the Headless Rider is a bad guy. We only wanna know what their deal is."

Mairu cut in. "You can stop there, Kuon."

"Huh?"

He turned back, cowed, as she continued, "Akane's on the

broadcasting committee at school, see? And one of the older kids on the committee vanished not that long ago."

"…"

"So that was two consecutive things you said that were very inconsiderate. Not that *I* mind, personally," she said.

Kuon broke into a cold sweat.

"…Yes, my upperclassman was a huge fan of the Headless Rider," Akane said. "But I didn't want to make things awkward, so I chose not to say anything about how I actually know the rider."

Her face drifted downward, and her expression was grave. "But… then that girl just disappeared…and everyone imagines all kinds of crazy things and says them like they're true…"

She was thinking back on the memory of her schoolmate about a week ago, when she met her during spring vacation.

"Hey, Akane. I think I might finally get to meet the Headless Rider!"

The girl had been the student president in elementary school. She was famous around school for her obsession with the Headless Rider.

Akane would have been happy to introduce her, but to do so would mean getting her family involved, and that was something she wanted to avoid at all costs.

"And if I get to be friends with the Headless Rider, Akane, I'll introduce you sometime!"

Only a few days after that, the upperclassman who had been kind and considerate to Akane when she was feeling down—and was to be her fellow student at the new middle school after spring vacation—went missing.

From what Akane understood, she'd been classified as a runaway with the police, but there hadn't been any news of the girl showing up.

The news trickled around the school in a similar fashion, and it was soon the talk of the entire student body.

"The Headless Rider abducted her into its shadow," the absurd rumors went.

But everyone living in Ikebukuro knew that the Headless Rider was indeed real.

It hadn't been seen in around half a year, but anyone who had witnessed it even once would come to the same conclusion: *That is not something of this world.*

A motorcycle that made no sound. Shadow that writhed and exuded something like smoke. There was no room to classify the urban legend of the Headless Rider as a simple folklore tale once you had seen these things for yourself.

Which is why a rumor like that could grow legs and spread throughout the school so quickly and effectively.

To Akane, whose life had been saved by the Headless Rider before, it was very difficult to watch the urban legend be cast in such dark and ominous terms. But no one was going to believe her if she claimed, "I was saved by the Headless Rider once!" And in order to explain it in enough detail to be believable, she would have to talk about her family background.

Akane was smart enough to know that would not make *anyone* happy.

So she held her tongue at school, pretending not to hear any of the gossip, and swore to herself deep down that she would investigate and get to the bottom of the disappearance herself.

This was the mindset she was in when she overheard Kuon, Yahiro, and Mairu talking at the gym—and she couldn't help but jump in to defend the honor of the Headless Rider—and now she was paying the price of Kuon's unnecessary attention.

"So what are you going to do?"

"…I'm going to go look for her."

"Look for her…by yourself? Seriously?"

"I can't leave it to the police," she said gloomily but firmly.

"If you're going to such lengths, you must really like this girl, huh? Or are you just that confident that the Headless Rider didn't do it?" asked Kuon, not shy in the least about getting into her business.

"Well…," she murmured, looking away.

"Look, we're not gonna do you wrong. Just tell us more about the Headless Rider! If there's some mistake going on, you should help clear it up. And if we know it's all mistaken, we can help spread the word that the rider's one of the good guys. Cool?"

"…"

Akane stared at the green-haired boy with suspicion, despite his gaping grin.

"Hey, you shouldn't be picking on poor little girls."

"Agagagagah!"

Mairu ground her fists against the sides of his head again, causing him to shriek. "Everyone has things they'd rather not talk about. Take a hint and be cool!"

"Owwww... But...but I'm curious," he protested.

Meanwhile, Yahiro had recovered from his funk. He approached Akane and said, "All right, if you don't want to talk, we won't ask about the Headless Rider anymore."

"...I'm sorry, thanks," she said, more in gratitude than apology, and bowed her head. But she seemed to view Yahiro as being slightly more trustworthy than Kuon, because she added, "You would know if you ever shared a conversation...that the Headless Rider isn't a bad person at all."

"I believe you."

"Huh?"

"Not being human doesn't mean you're bad," said Yahiro, with a strangely self-effacing grin.

Akane found that mystifying, but his response cheered her up. "Thank you!" She beamed. "I agree! It seems like everyone's getting the wrong idea...about the Headless Rider..." Then she paused, and this time she was the one wearing a self-effacing smile. "And about Shizuo..."

"Huh?"

"Oh, er, I'm sorry. That was just me talking to myself!" Akane said.

Mairu broke her silence with a smack of her fist against her palm. "Ah, that's right! The Headless Rider is friends with Shizuo, too!"

Yahiro's heart began to beat faster.

Shizuo? Is that...?

But Kuon reacted before Yahiro could speak his question out loud. "Whoa! Are you serious?! You mean, like, *the* Shizuo?! Shizuo Heiwajima!"

"Yeah, him. Oh, you know him?"

"Of course! Kuronuma tells me stories about him all the time. And I did see him throw a vending machine one time! Wait, so you're saying the Headless Rider knows Shizuo Heiwajima, too?! For real?"

"Aocchi doesn't tell you anything about stuff like that, then?" Mairu reacted with surprise.

Meanwhile, Yahiro's previous downcast mood had done a one-eighty into fierce excitement.

Shizuo Heiwajima.

Threw a vending machine.

That must be it!

It's him!

When searching for urban legends of Ikebukuro online, that was a name that appeared again and again. They called him the "Fighting Automaton," and he was often listed next to the Headless Rider as one of the "living urban legends of Ikebukuro."

And his name pops up here, right in this conversation! But why? Is it because they're both urban legends? he wondered, then shook his head. *No. This isn't the time to think about this stuff.*

Yahiro steadied his breath and said to Akane, "I'll help you find your friend."

"...Huh?" Her eyes were wide at this unexpected offer.

She wasn't the only one surprised at this. Kuon looked just as stunned, and Mairu was grinning at this development as though she found it quite entertaining.

"I want to know what the Headless Rider is like. If they're not a bad person, like you say, I would like to help prove that. And to do that, I'd like to hear what this schoolmate of yours who's obsessed with the rider has to say."

Well, I said it, no taking that back. I'm okay—I didn't lie. I didn't...right?

This was the perfect chance for Yahiro to find out more about not just the Headless Rider but this mysterious Shizuo Heiwajima person as well. Yes, he was worried for the sake of the missing girl, and he wanted to help this Akane girl, too, making it more of a "two birds, one stone" situation. Would it be duplicitous of him not to mention what the second bird was?

No. It doesn't matter. Besides, I really do want to know: Is it possible to be a monster and not be hated by others?

...In any case, the missing girl is clearly the biggest worry here. It's obvious what's most important of all.

Despite the oddly guilty feeling in the back of his head, Yahiro kept it hidden. He really did want to help find the missing girl. He was sure it was the right thing to do for someone else; he just couldn't be perfectly confident about it.

"..."

Akane said nothing but glanced at Mairu. It was the look of someone unsure of a new and unfamiliar person who is seeking reassurance.

Mairu gave her a big thumbs-up and said, "Good idea, right? Kuru and I will help, too!" Then she turned that thumbs-up toward Kuon and added, "And you can go and ask Aocchi's gang for help!"

Kuon was the one most surprised by this.

"Wha—? Hey—I have to help, too? And get Kuronuma involved and everything?"

"Nobody's forcing you. But you know what? You're not really the kind of person who says, 'Hey, amateurs like us should stay out of trouble and leave this to the police,' or, 'Why should I bother?' are you?"

The implicit message in her tone and look was clear: *I know you love sticking your head into trouble like this.*

That was, at the very least, *part* of Kuon's personality. He smiled back at the girl who was his senior at both school and dojo, cheek twitching, and simply shook his head.

"I'm amazed you can be so confident about that, given we've only met a few times," he said.

"My brother's really good at that sort of thing. Must be in our blood," Mairu said, cackling. She tried to reassure Akane by saying, "Look, it'll be fine. I'm sure she's just acting out and running away, and we'll find her safe and sound."

"But…" Akane was still worried.

"Now, now, you can worry that you're placing a burden on us later!" Mairu said. "Me and these boys are doing what we want because we want to, and we know there's a possibility it might lead to danger. You have to recognize that sometimes older folks are simply going to do something nice for you, Akane!"

Kuon interjected, "Well, I'm not doing it of *my* own free will…"

Mairu leered back at him. "So you're not getting involved? I'll just ask Aocchi myself, then."

"…No, I'll do it. Might as well see this thing through," he grumbled reluctantly.

Akane considered these statements some more and seemed to arrive at a resolution. A newfound look of commitment entered her eyes, and she bowed.

"Thank you very much… I appreciate your help!" she said, clenching the rod she was holding. "But...if it starts looking dangerous, please stop right away. The last thing I want is for any of you to be in danger..."

Kuon shrugged his shoulders and teased, "Whoa, whoa, whoa, if anyone here is likely to be in danger, it's the youngest of us all, isn't that right?"

"Kuon, I wouldn't underestimate Akane if I were you. She might only be starting middle school, but she's a rising star in the Rakuei Jodo Dojo!"

"For real?! Wow...okay, then the person here who needs to be the most careful is Yahiro," he decided, slapping Yahiro on the back.

"Uh, y-yeah, I'll be careful." The other boy smiled, feeling conflicted. He tried to change the subject by asking Akane, "So, uh...anyway, what's the name of this girl who went missing?"

She took a deep breath, let it out, and stated, "Tatsugami. Her name is Ai Tatsugami."

"Huh?"

Tatsugami.

That had a familiar sound to it.

Yahiro started wondering if it was just a common name around the Ikebukuro area, but he quickly came to a more logical conclusion.

She was related to the Tatsugami girl that *he* knew.

And Yahiro wasn't the only one arriving at that thought. Kuon inclined his head slightly and said, "Isn't there...a Tatsugami in our class, too? Are they related?"

Yahiro couldn't say for certain. "Well...they might be, but we can't be sure yet."

The missing girl named Tatsugami was a huge fan of the Headless Rider. It would be ridiculous to assume they had no connection.

Yahiro felt his classmate's warning rise to the surface of his mind.

"Don't dig too deeply into the Headless Rider."

He was getting dragged into something.

That much, Yahiro the coward was certain of.

But there was no way to stop at this point.

Struggling against the cloud of anxiety storming in his chest, the timid boy decided that he would continue onward.

♂♀

After that, Yahiro observed Kuon performing his gym training, took a pamphlet, and went home.

Kuon and Akane left when they were done, too, which left just Mairu behind, waiting for her sister to arrive in the waiting room.

"I gotta tell Kuru about this. Starting tomorrow, we're going on a manhunt with the Secret Society of Hot-Blooded Cold-Blooded Ikebukuro Detectives' Secret Society. Whoops, I said 'secret society' twice. Oh, well, it doesn't matter."

She was sitting in a chair in the waiting room, kicking her legs and passing the time by coming up with names for the impromptu group, feeling excited about the whole thing, when a voice from the hallway called out, "Hey, Mairu."

"Oh! Instructor Mikage! Good evening!"

It was Mikage Sharaku.

She was the daughter of Rakuei Gym's president, an instructor with a distinctly athletic appearance. Mairu had known her since joining the gym, and they often spoke to each other not as teacher and student but like friends of very different ages.

She asked Mairu, "Those boys you were talking to earlier—are they friends of yours?"

"Who, Kuon and Mizuchi? They're students at Raira. They said they just started school today."

"Hmm…were they practicing?"

"Huh? Well, Kuon's been a member of Rakuei Dojo for years. He was going to the Takadanobaba location, he said. What's up, Mikage?! Do you think he's oozing with potential or something?! Is he like Mr. Kisa, where he could potentially be the second coming of Traugott?!" Mairu asked excitedly. She hadn't seen Kuon practicing for herself.

But Mikage shook her head. "Kuon is the one with the green hair, right? Well, he's practicing our style. So it was clear from a glance that he'd been one of our pupils for a while…"

Then she paused, thought for a moment, and asked, "The boy who was just watching. His name was Mizuchi, you said?"

"Yep… What about him? Oh, is he your type, Mikage?"

"Don't be stupid. That's not it… I mean, has *he* been practicing something?"

"Hmm? Has he? I didn't ask. I would assume that Kuon would've brought it up if he was aware," said Mairu, taken aback that it was Yahiro the older instructor was curious about. "What is it about him? He seemed pretty reserved to me."

"Did you look at his hands?"

"His hands? Um, I guess I didn't. What was it about Mizuchi's hands?"

Mikage considered her answer carefully, then laid down an ultimatum.

"What I'm going to say to you now cannot get passed to his ears or anyone else's. Except for Kururi, I suppose, since I'm sure you'll tell her no matter what. That's fine but nobody else. Can you keep it to yourself?"

Mairu stopped kicking her legs and stared at her instructor's solemn face with a smile. "Yeah. I promise."

"Thank you. I wouldn't want him to suffer any strange rumors."

Mikage put a coin in the waiting room's vending machine and hit the button for a sports drink with a blend of amino acids. She continued, "He was sitting all prim and proper, watching very keenly, but I just happened to catch a glimpse of his hands resting on his knees..."

She picked up the canned beverage that emerged from the machine.

"They were all scarred to hell."

"Scarred?"

True, if you practiced karate by striking those posts wrapped with rough straw rope, it was easy to scar up your fingers. But Mairu couldn't see why that would be such cause for concern.

"You could get scars like that from having a cat and getting bitten, though," she said.

"...Yes, that's true," Mikage admitted. "Those were definitely teeth marks. But not cat teeth."

"Hwa?"

"I only know this from personal experience...," Mikage said.

Mairu looked at the hands holding the sports drink and realized there were a number of old scars there—not the kind you picked up from regular martial arts training.

"Those are human teeth marks," she finished.

"...Like someone bit him?" Mairu wondered.

Mikage shook her head. "When you punch someone in the mouth and break their teeth, the jagged parts will stick into your skin sometimes."

"..."

"And when you keep punching and punching and punching after they're broken, it guarantees more wounds. It's not a smart move because of the risk of infection. There are much easier ways to take out an opponent if you're that much stronger than them."

Mikage envisioned the hands she had seen, the details that it had etched upon her mind. Her expressionless face hid the stew of complex emotions behind it. The conclusion was clear.

"Those scars on Mizuchi's hands... Those were put there by broken teeth."

"...You're sure?"

"And with so many...I can't even imagine how many people's teeth he's broken."

Mikage took a sip of the drink. She smiled weakly and muttered to herself.

"It gave me the shivers."

♂♀

Takadanobaba—Kuon's apartment

"I'm home."

Kuon Kotonami's first destination back at home was his elder sister's room in the back.

Moving boxes were stacked almost to the ceiling near the doorway. They were split into separate towers of opened and unopened things.

Between the towers were glimpses of the floor, upon which were piled emptied teacups and plates, along with neatly arranged chopsticks.

"Oh! You ate all your food today, Sis," he said, picking up the dishes, but he was not actually addressing someone present in the room. "For being so regular about taking showers, you sure do hate eating food in the kitchen. I don't understand the difference."

He took the dishes back to the sink, grumbling to himself all the while. Aside from his sister's room, the apartment was neat and tidy, without so much as a spot of mold around the sink.

Kuon fastidiously washed the dishes, then sat on the sofa in the living room and opened the laptop resting on the table there. Then he

turned on the TV and used his spare hand to thumb down the screen
of his smartphone.

"And now…"

The evening news program was on the TV. He put the phone to his ear.

"Hi there."

"_____"

"I know, I know. I called because I have some intel for you,"
Kuon said to the person on the other end, grinning to himself. He
announced his findings. "Nope, nothing crazy about the entrance ceremony. In fact, I had the craziest appearance. Lotta Goody Two-shoes
at Raira Academy, it seems like."

"_____"

"A lot of other stuff happened today, though. I found an interesting
pawn."

Unlike the simpering, polite smile he wore before the class earlier
today, the grin on Kuon's face now was somehow cold.

"Would you believe this? A guy who moved all the way here from
Akita, just to see the Headless Rider!"

"_____"

"No, it's true! See? That's the kind of person we've been looking for,
right? And he seemed pretty naive and trusting, so I'm sure we can get
him to do what we want. Like, I was seriously ready to be his friend."

"_____"

"I'm just kidding. Do I look like a guy who has friends?" said Kuon,
shrugging. "His name's Yahiro Mizuchi…and he's got all *kinds* of gifts."

Kuon envisioned the face of the peon he'd found that day and narrowed his eyes until they were like a snake's.

"And because I was walking around with him, I found a number of
other things I could potentially harvest."

♂♀

Rakuei Gym

Now that Mikage had brought up Yahiro, she turned to the topic of
the other student.

"By the way, what's up with that Kuon boy? He seemed to be taking his practice pretty seriously. I bet if my brother or dad see him, they'll yell, 'Dye your hair black!' Everybody's so old-fashioned around here."

"Hmm. Well, I think it's fun, so I'm fine with him staying green," Mairu replied. She thought it over a bit. "I guess he's a bad guy. The kind who uses others rather than doing stuff himself. I'm betting he's here at this dojo so he can learn the minimum of self-defense. Just in case it's a necessity. Oh, and I said, 'it's a,' not 'Iza.' Although…speaking of Iza, I think this guy's the same type of person."

"…If he's like your brother, then he's more of a pure scumbag than a bad guy," murmured Mikage with a wistful look. "And what's his connection to that Mizuchi boy, then?"

"He said they were friends, but I think he's using him. Mizuchi definitely seemed very naive. I just don't know what he's using him *for*."

"…I'm amazed that you can be so friendly with a guy you describe this way, Mairu."

After that, Mairu told Mikage about what she'd discussed with the boys. When it came to the conversation with Akane, Mikage laughed.

"Ohhh, so they've decided to go searching for Akane's upperclassman."

"Yeah. I hope they find her…"

"Well, let's hope those boys don't get any funny ideas about messing with Akane. I assume they have no idea about her background," Mikage said, placing her can into the trash.

But Mairu said, "I'm sure Mizuchi doesn't know. I'm not so sure about Kuon."

"?"

"If he's hanging around with Aocchi, I'm certain he has to know about the Awakusu-kai."

♂♀

Kuon's apartment

"Yep, Akane Awakusu. The granddaughter of Dougen Awakusu, leader of the Awakusu-kai!"

"_____"

"Hilarious, right? The pampered little daughter of the Awakusu, claiming she has connections to the Headless Rider," Kuon said to his phone partner with delight, wearing an expression he was careful never to show in Akane's presence. "Well, when Yahiro said he'd help her find this person, I wondered what was up, but the end result should be pretty entertaining. Anyway, the girl that Akane Awakusu wants to find is named—let's see...Ai Tatsugami..."

"____, _____?"

"Yeah, I assume they have to be related. The journalist who disappeared not long ago was an Aya Tatsugami, right?"

"_____"

Kuon nodded. "Yeah, if you could look into that, I'd appreciate it. I don't have connections to any publishers, of course. Oh, and this might be just a coincidence...but there's a Tatsugami in my class, too. Seems standoffish, but she's pretty cute."

"_____"

"No, no, nothing like that. But if she's related, too, that'd be the jackpot. Anyway, I want to be careful about this. It could end up involving millions of yen, maybe tens of millions. If there's any bidding competition...it'd be Kuronuma, I guess. He knows everything I'm up to, after all."

Then Kuon asked the person on the other end, "What's up with you, then? Anything interesting happening?"

"_____"

"Uh...hang on! Who got out of prison? A big name? Dollars? Or Yellow Scarves? Huh? Blue Squares?!"

Like a snake that had just spotted prey, Kuon's eyes sparkled with excitement. But that gleam clouded over within moments.

"_____"

"Former Blue Square, now a Yellow Scarf... Horada...?"

"_____"

"Okay...So he's finally out, huh...? Horada... _The_ Horada...Horada, Horada..."

His face went blank, and then his head inclined a bit with indecision.

"...Sorry, who's that?"

INTERMISSION
Online Rumors (2)

On the Ikebukuro information site IkeNew! Version I.KEBU.KUR.O

Popular Post: [Urban Legend Resumes] Turns out the serial disappearances in Ikebukuro are being done by the Headless Rider!

"Is the Headless Rider the common factor linking the Ikebukuro serial disappearances?" (Rehosted from *Daily Baboo* online site)

Has the darkness in Ikebukuro finally made itself known?

Tokyo is stunned by a recent situation that might make you wonder about that.

Young people in the Ikebukuro area have been going missing since last December, and now whispers are swirling that the disappearances might be related to the Headless Rider.

They say the missing and runaways share one key trait.

What is that trait? That they were pursuing the identity of the Headless Rider.

The Headless Rider is a mysterious being that has been seen countless times over at least the last two decades.

It rides a motorcycle that makes no engine noise and transforms into a headless horse. The rider creates shadow from its own body that it can control at will.

The only suitable term for such a being is *urban legend*, but in recent times, up until six months ago, it was a common enough sight that residents of Ikebukuro were regularly capturing it on their phone cameras.

But since those eyewitness accounts dropped off, some young folks have turned into fervent "devotees" of the Headless Rider.

To a person, they told others in their vicinity that they "might be able to meet the Headless Rider," immediately before they disappeared.

Last month, a writer for a local print magazine even disappeared after claiming that she was going to "meet with an influential intel provider."

(Omitted)

There are also rumors about connections between the Headless Rider and local yakuza. Even the police are looking into the rider as a person of interest in the string of disappearances.

(Omitted)

—*(The rest of this article can be read at the original link)*

Comment from IkeNew! *Administrator*

First, they vanished, I thought, now they're doing the vanishing.
For the people who have gone missing to show up safe and sound, I pray.

Admin: Rira Tailtooth Zaiya

♂♀

A selection of representative twits from the social network Twittia

You remember how the Headless Rider had a bounty at one point? Well, that sure got canceled in a hurry. Suspicious, yeah? I bet the government was involved.

→I think the police scolded the person who set up the bounty.

→Common sense should tell you that the police would be mad about it. They probably took that into account before placing the bounty. It's suspicious because they retracted it right away.

→Never underestimate Max Sandshelt's love for messy drama.

A kid from my college is missing. It's crazy. They've been a huge fanatic of the Headless Rider since they were a kid. Isn't that wild? It's freaky. I think I'm happier that they're gone now. What a creep.

→That's really inappropriate to say about someone who's gone missing.

→So? I can say what I want. Don't pop into a stranger's thread. Who are you?

→Oh yeah? I can reply what I want, too. You're just as annoying.

→Then don't look at my twits, idiot. Go die! Die, die, die, die.

→According to your past posts, you've driven drunk. And it seems like you're cheating at school, too? I'll go ahead and report that, Mr. Raira Freshman.

→I'm sorry, I was just joking. I'm not a student at Raira University, either. Please don't contact the school, you'll only be bothering them.

* (The original poster was later expelled from Raira University, then prosecuted for a separate matter. The case is still in court.)

Before the magazine writer went missing, they said they were meeting an influential intel provider. But who would be able to provide info about the Headless Rider?

→I've seen the rider carrying a guy in a white lab coat on their back seat.

→Rumor is that's a black market doctor.

→Maybe Shizuo Heiwajima? You see him around it, too.

→So it's like 1) Shizuo gets pissed 2) throws them really far away 3) they're never seen again?

→Holy crap.

→Wasn't there some info dealer who would talk with the Headless Rider now and then?

→"info dealer" lol

→I'm serious! There was a guy!

→You mean the one in the black fur-lined coat? Haven't seen him lately.

CHAPTER 3

CHAPTER 3 A
The Destroyer

There is a demon in Ikebukuro.

This is a story that anyone living long enough in Ikebukuro will hear.

And those who visit the busy shopping area around the station every day will know it is not simply rumor.

Guardrails torn off by force.

Light poles yanked out of the ground.

Street signs broken in half.

Vending machines warped and shattered.

If you have seen any of these disquieting signs of violence, then you have almost certainly seen the work of one specific human being.

Shizuo Heiwajima.

He is a man distinguished by his everyday wear of a bartender's outfit, flashy bleached blond hair, and sunglasses.

He makes a living by collecting debts from people who owe money to various hookup sites, prostitution schemes, and hostess clubs, and he can be seen in Ikebukuro's active commercial areas around Sunshine and Sixtieth Floor Street on a daily basis.

That description alone makes him sound like a man who merely has a rough-and-tumble job, but he truly is undoubtedly worthy of the title of the "strongest man in Ikebukuro," as childish as that appellation may sound.

To attempt to catalogue every legend told about Shizuo Heiwajima would be a never-ending fool's errand.

The man who swings vending machines one-handed.
The man who rips loose guardrails one-handed.
The man who cuts cars in two with street signs.
The man who got run over by a dump truck and stood up perfectly fine.
The man who lifted a refrigerator as a little boy.
The man who keeps a tiger as a pet.
The man who loves vanilla milkshakes.
The man who has a Russian assassin for an apprentice.
The man who can only be stabbed a millimeter deep.
The man who repels bullets with his flesh.
The man who loves fruit jelly desserts with ice cream.
The man who destroyed an entire building by himself.
The man who wiped out a motorcycle gang by swinging a light pole.
The man who bends metal pipes out of shape when they hit him.
The man who can only be pierced with a ballpoint pen made by Nebula.
The man who kicks cars like soccer balls.
The man who crushes coal into diamonds with the palm of his hand.
The man who loves flan.
The man who is the brother of star actor Yuuhei Hanejima.
The man who can chuck someone over a high-rise building.
The man who loves pancakes topped with syrup.
The man who loves sweets, basically.

It was impossible to know which of these rumors were true and which were made up, but everyone who was familiar with Shizuo would believe they *could* be true.

One theory said the abrupt end to the serial slashings that momentarily plunged Ikebukuro into a paralyzing terror was because the slasher tried to mess with Shizuo Heiwajima and got absolutely pulverized for it.

Floating around on the Internet was footage of him throwing vending machines and swinging around light poles. But most people who watched those videos merely thought, *That's some well-done, sneaky editing.*

It was true that he was the brother of the famous actor Yuuhei Hanejima; because of that, perhaps it was easier for skeptics to assume that any unbelievable videos were fakes cooked up by the TV network.

However, there was one legend in particular that arose in conversation again and again, especially in recent days.

The man who is friends with the Headless Rider.

This was not a rumor that was simply attempting to tie one urban legend to another without foundation. Shizuo Heiwajima had been seen several times accompanying the Headless Rider.

The connection between these two legends was akin to a famous soccer player and baseball player hanging out in public and having a great time. Those who were familiar with both legends would find this sight shocking and sear it into their brains.

And now that the Headless Rider is gone—the other living legend of Ikebukuro is about to reach a major turning point.

♂♀

A parlor in Ikebukuro—evening

Inside a department store in Ikebukuro, there was an establishment called a "fruit parlor," a kind of café serving fruit-based dishes.

Most of the customers inside were women, but there were some male visitors who appeared to be on their way home from work. Two, in particular, did not look like typical office workers.

A man in a bartender's getup was eating an extravagantly assembled parfait with pieces of mango carved to look like roses, while another man with dreadlocks was eating a panini sandwich garnished with seasonal vegetables.

"So you wanna get a license?" asked Tom Tanaka, the man with the dreads, pausing in the middle of his sandwich.

Shizuo Heiwajima, the man in the bartender uniform, explained, "Yeah. You've got a bunch of licenses, right? What are they again?"

"Uh, let's see... I've got my real estate license, for one. Then there's the kanji and English qualifications, although those are both just second rank. Plus, there's a surveyor's license, bookkeeping license, a third-rank secretarial aptitude certificate..."

Tom continued listing off qualifications he possessed, as Shizuo listened with great reverence. "Wow...that's incredible."

They had recently finished their work quota for the day. The sun had already set. Normally at this hour, they'd report in at their work and go home, but Shizuo said he wanted to talk about something, so they decided to get a bite to eat and hash it out.

"Basically, I was thinking that if I had a bunch of qualifications, I wouldn't have to worry about putting food on the table... If I weren't working this job, I'd probably have even more by now," Tom said.

"Are there any licenses you think I could get pretty easily?" asked Shizuo. He had never talked about this before, so Tom was taken aback.

"What's up with you? Are you switching jobs or something?"

"Er, no, I'm happy with the job. I'm not thinking of a different line of work...but I dunno. I feel like I want something that makes me feel more confident about myself..."

"..."

Shizuo Heiwajima possessed brute strength and toughness that surpassed the boundaries of humanity. As his work superior, Tom knew that as well as anyone.

But he did not say, *As long as you have that monster strength, you'll be fine.*

He knew that Shizuo did not actually desire his incredibly violent power.

"Well, look. I know the company we work for isn't exactly on the up-and-up. So it's always possible that it might go up in smoke one day," Tom said. "So...there are lots of qualifications out there, but quite a few of them require a number of years or a job in that field. Hang on a sec."

He took out his smartphone and started looking up stuff online.

"There are lots out there if you just want civilian qualifications.

Jewelry coordinator, nature guide… Oooh, you can be certified as a world heritage site expert?"

"I don't know much about world heritage sites…"

"Well, normally you'd know what you want to do before you start trying to earn qualifications. So is there anything you want to do with your life outside this job?" Tom asked directly.

Shizuo thought it over. "If I knew that for sure, I'd be able to narrow it down. The thing is, I just can't tell what it is I want to do with my future."

"Forget about now, then. What did you want to do as a kid?"

"Huh?"

"It's important to get back to your roots with this sort of thing. You must've had a dream or two when you were a little boy," Tom said.

Shizuo thought hard again.

Dreams. My dreams. Hey, yeah, there was *something.*

After another several moments, Shizuo recalled what it was he'd written in his elementary school graduation essay.

"Yeah…that's right. That's it."

"You remember something?"

Shizuo nodded, reminiscing on his past, and said, "Yeah. I think I wanted to be a *detective*."

"…Uh-huh."

A detective.

It was hard to tell if Shizuo would be good at this job or not, Tom decided.

In having this dream from when he was in elementary school, he would certainly have been in admiration of the detectives from movies and comic books, not real-life private investigators who mostly looked for evidence of marriage infidelity.

But even fictional detectives came in a few varieties.

There were the cerebral types, who used rigorous logic based on available clues to uncover the true killer.

The combative types, who traipsed around various crime scenes for evidence and occasionally had to fight off attackers.

And some characters like Sherlock Holmes had elements of both. It was hard to narrow down the concept of a detective to a single, concise image.

Honestly, a fighting detective like the kind you saw in movies might be the perfect occupation for Shizuo, but this was sadly not the world of cinema. Tom had a hard time envisioning Shizuo performing tedious gumshoe work and searching for missing pets.

But if he had a cerebral partner, then you might have something interesting...

Cerebral, huh?

Tom thought of every person he knew who might be considered smart and thoughtful.

One of them was a certain information broker, but he banished that thought from his mind as soon as it appeared.

Nope...anyone but him. I can't possibly see Shizuo and him working together as a team. They're not the kind of odd couple from the movies who bicker and get the job done. They're the kind that try to kill each other when they're in the same room... Plus, he's not in town anymore.

Meanwhile, Shizuo came to a conclusion of his own. "Okay...I think I get it, Tom. The reason that I've been able to stick to this job for so long is because, I think, it kind of fits with the concept of a detective that I wanted to be as a kid."

"Huh?"

Tom thought back on the job duties Shizuo had been performing here: finding people who had vanished without paying their debts or who, in some cases, turned and attacked the collectors tasked with tracking them down.

In fact, their job had just been a long string of these incidents. Tom smirked and shook his head.

"I don't think I like being reminded of how violent our job is..."

♂♀

Ikebukuro West Gate Park—thirty minutes later

On the way back to the office to report on the day's activities, Tom said, "I'm surprised you brought that topic up."

Shizuo seemed more serious than usual. "It's like...I've been thinking that I really need to change myself..."

"Oh yeah?"

"Today was the Raira entrance ceremony, it seemed like. I saw the new students showing up there, their eyes sparkling with new possibilities."

"Now that you mention it, I saw a lot more uniforms today," Tom noted. He glanced around the park.

Of course, there were hardly any uniforms to be seen at this hour, but there were plenty of young people all the same. There was a healthy variety, from normal-looking youth to surly punks, but the gangsters dressed in matching colors that had been so frequent in recent years were all but gone.

Shizuo observed the changing nature of the city and said wistfully, "Ever since that fleabrain got lost, it feels like this place has finally chilled out. It's been like this for over a year, so I'm feeling like I should finally get my act together..."

"That's a good point. Although those twins are still as wild as ever."

"Yeah, but they don't cause trouble in the same way," said Shizuo, right as one of the two girls appeared.

"Oh, speak of the devil. Wonder if the other one's still at Rakuei Gym?" Tom muttered, recognizing Kururi Orihara—but something was strange about her.

There was a group of unsavory-looking young men in her presence. It looked less like a pickup attempt than a very forceful quest to lure her somewhere else.

"Hang on. I thought idiots like that were lying low these days," Tom grumbled. But his partner was already walking over. "Ah, hey, Shizuo..."

"No, see, we're not saying you have to make out with all of us or anything."

"We just wanna celebrate our buddy for getting outta jail. And every party needs at least one pretty girl, you know?"

"You're *exactly* his type, from what I understand," claimed the hoodlums surrounding Kururi.

She exhaled and, in a quiet but firm voice, said, "...No..." [I decline.]

"Nah, it doesn't work like that. You don't get to back out."

"Listen, how would you rather this play out? We can drag you kicking and screaming into our car, or you can come along and enjoy yourself! I think you know which would be better, right?"

Behind them was a man leaning against a stone pillar with his back turned toward them. That was probably their "friend" who had just gotten out of prison.

But it was a different man who entered the scene and said, "Hey, knock it off."

"Uhhh? Who the hell are you? A bartender?"

The ruffians immediately turned sour looks on the man in the recognizable outfit who had just appeared.

"I know this girl. Would you mind not dragging her off?"

Their best attempt at intimidating stares was easily ignored. Irritated, the young men took more direct—and shortsighted—action.

"Pretending to be a hero ain't in fashion anymore, idiot," one of them said, and dumped the contents of his plastic bottle over the man in the bartender suit.

That action alone made it clear to everyone around that these young men were not local residents. Any proper Ikebukuro citizen would know exactly what kind of fire they were playing with.

Orange juice poured out of the mouth of the bottle and splattered across the hair and clothes of the man trying to defuse the situation.

Kururi quietly backed away. The man with the dreads who was watching from a distance scowled, then put his hands together in a prayer for the young men.

Without realizing the mistake they had made, one of the thugs turned back to their newly freed buddy and said, "Mr. Horada! Mr. Horada! It's cool if we execute this guy, right?"

The man he called Horada slowly got to his feet and murmured, "Well, well, you guys got no patience, huh? Look, I don't wanna get tossed right back into the joint. Go soft on him. Just break his arms and legs, but not bad enough that he di..."

Only then did Horada actually turn his face to see the man they were talking about.

All time froze for him.

"............"

"Uh...Mr. Horada?"

He was standing there, pale as a sheet, his mouth flapping silently.

But no sooner had they called out his name than the man in the bartender's outfit grabbed one of the punks by his face.

"Hey...you wanna know something?"

"?! ?! ?!"

The young man flailed his limbs, panicked by the sudden pain and constriction. It was like some giant vise was pinching the sides of his head.

The man continued to the uncomprehending ruffians, "People...can die just like that. I suppose someone could have a heart attack from shock and die, just because someone dumped a bottle of water over his head. You know that?"

"Gah...*gurk*..."

"H-hey, man! What the hell do you think you're doing?!"

The others tried to grapple with the man, but he did not budge the tiniest bit. It was as if he were a giant tree with burly roots in the ground.

"And that would mean you tried to kill me...right?"

"Wh-what the hell is he saying...?" stammered the panicking young men, looking to Horada for help.

But Horada himself was shivering, knees knocking like a baby deer, in an attempt to escape. "H...Hei...Heiwajima..."

Behind him, Shizuo Heiwajima bellowed, "Meaning...that you can't complain if I kill you back!"

He hurled the boy against Horada's back.

"Guhf?!"

Tom watched the carnage unfold and muttered to himself, "In the past, he would have tossed that guy just from messing with Kururi in the first place..."

One after the other, the street punks were getting slammed to the ground. The man freed from prison was trying to crawl away in escape.

Tom shrugged. "I guess this counts as progress."

CHAPTER 3 B
The Challenger

Raira Academy—the next day

It was the second day of Raira Academy's school year, but classes were not in session yet.

This day was mainly for orientation purposes—touring the school facilities, introducing the student committees and club activities, and so on. Each class would then elect its own officers and representatives.

Until a few years ago, the student committee roles were decided on the first day, but the school decided that they needed more time for explanations of the roles, so that was moved to the second day of school.

Yahiro nominated himself for the library committee. No one else joined him, so he was made the representative by default. The first activity after school that day was a round of introductions, then the selection of the chair and vice chair, followed by future activities, and then the rotation of who would manage the library.

By the time all these steps were done, the sun was setting. The sky was red and vivid through the windows when Yahiro returned to the classroom.

There was also a familiar girl present in the corner of the room.

"Did you…wait for me here?"

"Well, I had nothing else to do," admitted Himeka Tatsugami brusquely. "How was the library committee?"

"Uh, I was nervous, but they all seemed nice. And the committee chairman seemed nice, too."

"Is the library committee chairman the cool-looking one with the glasses?"

"Yeah, that's right."

With those pleasantries out of the way, Himeka launched right into the topic she really wanted to discuss. "So anyway."

"What?"

"Should we continue our discussion from yesterday now?"

"Isn't that why you were waiting?" asked Yahiro, with no apparent sign of irony or sarcasm.

Himeka let out a little sigh. "You really are strange."

"I am? Well…I'll be careful of that. Thanks for letting me know."

"That's not really something you should be thanking me for…," she murmured, not letting the confusion show on her face. But that was as far as she let that topic go. "In that case, I guess I should ask—why are you chasing after the Headless Rider?"

"…Ah. Right," Yahiro said, pausing to collect his thoughts. "I want to figure something out. If I'm a normal person…or if I'm a monster."

"Huh?"

"They called me a monster back where I'm from. I didn't have any friends in elementary school. The only people who wanted anything from me were the kind who would just walk up and start hitting me."

"…"

Although she was a bit confused by this, Himeka did not interrupt, choosing to wait for Yahiro to finish his story instead.

"But one day, someone came to the hot spring in the town and said to me, 'You're not a monster; you're an ordinary person'… He told me that there was a world I didn't know yet here in Ikebukuro."

"…And that's why you moved here?"

"Yeah. I wanted to see the wider world out there. I thought I was doomed to this life, but here in Tokyo, there are people far stranger than me leading ordinary lives and getting along fine…" Yahiro smiled awkwardly and admitted, "I thought, if I could see that for myself, I might be able to accept what I am in a different light. That's why I came to Ikebukuro."

*   *   *

"..."

Himeka had listened closely to what he said.

It was a strange story, but he didn't seem to be lying about it.

Yahiro claimed that people called him a monster, but nothing about his appearance suggested such a thing. While he was a bit eccentric, he wasn't some kind of alien freak who was clearly on a different plane of existence from the rest of humanity.

He must have suffered some extreme kind of bullying. Brutal and persistent hazing, pelted with rocks, treated like a beast.

Specifically, it was the scars on Yahiro's hands that convinced her of this. There were strange marks on the backs of both his hands. They had to be from the bullying he suffered.

So Himeka decided to believe his story for now. She was still skeptical about why he would be here to see Shizuo Heiwajima in particular, but for the time being, she decided that this boy was worth telling her situation.

"...Okay. I understand why you want to meet the Headless Rider."

"You do? I'm glad. I didn't think you would believe me," Yahiro said, relieved.

Himeka was quiet for a few moments, then went on, "But even then...I don't think you should chase after the rider or worship it."

"Will you, um...tell me why? Today this time?" Yahiro asked. He didn't want to force her to speak, but he'd told her his own secret, so it was worth a shot.

Himeka said, "Well, I promised. And even if I don't say it, the story will get out eventually, I'm sure..." She sighed in resignation and explained, "I have an older sister and a younger sister. I'm the middle child of three."

"Uh-huh."

"My older sister is a journalist for a local paper, and she's been pursuing the Headless Rider for a big story. And my younger sister, she's been obsessed with the Headless Rider ever since she was a little girl. She was always big on dreaming and fantasies, so I'm sure that's why she was fond of a legend who might as well have fallen out of a comic book."

She stopped there for a while. Eventually, she seemed to reach a moment of determination, inhaled, and continued the story.

"They...both went missing. On the same day."

"..."

"They were both worked up that morning. They said they were going to meet the *partner* of the Headless Rider... My older sister was going to have an interview for her article, and my younger sister was tagging along. And then they never came back," Himeka said, as simple as if reciting historical facts. "I think they got dragged into something. But it wasn't just them. The police kept asking about the Headless Rider when they talked to me, so I knew something was up. When I looked into it, I found out about more."

"More...people who went missing?"

"Yes. I know of at least seven. But I think there are many more."

"..."

Now it was Yahiro's turn to be silent.

The bit about the older sister was news to him, but he already had a guess about the younger sister. But how to bring that up now, without possibly hurting her feelings, made it difficult for Yahiro to mention that he knew her sister's name.

But then again...if I don't say anything, it'll be like I'm lying to her.

So he decided to go ahead and ask, "Um, is your younger sister's name...Ai Tatsugami, perhaps?"

"!"

Her reaction alone, before saying a single word, told him all he needed to know.

"How do you know...my sister's name?"

"Well, yesterday I met a girl in middle school...and she was talking about how a girl from her school went missing. And the girl's name was Ai Tatsugami, so I just had a hunch..."

"Oh...I see. That makes sense. If you live here, you don't need to go looking for the Headless Rider to hear stories like that."

"Um. Yeah. I'm sorry." Yahiro bowed.

Before he could continue the conversation, someone else burst into the classroom.

"Whatcha doin' here?"

*　　*　　*

It was a frivolous classmate with bright green hair.

"Um…"

"What do you want, Kotonami?" asked Yahiro, covering for Himeka, who didn't seem to remember the boy's name.

"Hey, c'mon. I told you to call me Kuon, remember?" he said, bubbly on the surface. But Himeka's eyes narrowed. She was clearly wary of him.

Sensing that potential hostility, Yahiro tried to smooth things over. "Oh, he took me to a martial arts gym yesterday. That's where I heard that story I was talking about."

Kuon latched on to that. "Oh, are you talking about what you heard from Akane? Were you curious because the girl had the same last name?"

"Uh. Yeah, that."

"Wow, really? You're just going to ask her directly to her face about that? Really?" Kuon exclaimed in disbelief. But despite the words, his tone wasn't accusatory. If anything, he seemed to be grateful to Yahiro for doing the heavy lifting and asking the awkward questions.

Yahiro didn't want her getting any suspicions about him. He hastily explained, "Kuon was there when we were talking yesterday…and we're supposed to be helping that girl find her friend from middle school. And since she had the same last name as you, I couldn't help but wonder."

She fixed him with a stare, then exhaled. "I'd prefer if you didn't get into our business…but neither that girl nor either of you have any idea what I'm going through, so I suppose it's not fair of me to be angry at you."

"Uh…sorry about this."

"No, I'm the one who owes you an apology. Sorry for making this awkward," she said, without changing expression.

That just made Yahiro feel even more guilty. Her family members were missing; she had to be a wreck on the inside. She'd probably locked her heart shut tight, which was why there was such little natural expression in her features, he presumed.

Himeka continued, "Well, I might as well explain to you, Kotonami…"

"Oh, call me Kuon. And I'll call you Himeka."

"I'm very sorry, Kotonami, but I do not want you to do that."

"Oh."

Undeterred by the interruption, Himeka returned to what she was about to say.

"My older and younger sisters both got involved with the Headless Rider and vanished."

"Huh? Two sisters?!"

Hmm? What was that? Yahiro wondered. Something felt strange about Kuon's surprise, but he couldn't tell what it was, so the thought soon slipped out of his mind.

"Yes. I told Yahiro earlier, so you can have him repeat it after this."

"Hang on. You'll call Yahiro by his first name? But you refuse to do it for me?!"

"Huh? For one thing, Yahiro is easier to say than Mizuchi. Plus, I said I didn't want *you* to call me by *my* first name..."

"But in either case, you clearly don't like me, right?"

As he listened to them bicker, Yahiro realized what it was that seemed off to him a moment earlier.

Oh, I get it. It's like...the way Kuon speaks...it's all deliberate. *All of it, overall.*

It seemed to Yahiro that Kuon was hiding what he truly felt behind his exterior. But then he admonished himself.

No, you dummy. Don't assume that. Maybe everyone in Tokyo is like this, and you're just not used to it yet...

In fact, even within Kuon's circle of acquaintances, almost none of them sensed a deliberate falsehood in his mannerisms.

But Yahiro was not mistaken in his assumption.

A small cross section of others, including the Orihara sisters and Aoba Kuronuma, were fully aware of this tendency of Kuon's and understood just what he really was.

Despite the second interjection, Himeka soldiered on with her warning for the boys.

"I don't know about this girl you met, although it's nice that she's worried for my sister. But you understand that the Headless Rider is dangerous now, I trust. You should stay away—for your own good."

"Yeah…I get that," said Yahiro, his first words in quite a while, "but even then…I don't think that girl's going to stop searching."

"…Why do you say that?"

"She said, 'The Headless Rider's not a bad person.' Strangely enough…it sounded like the girl knew the rider. But whatever her story was, I didn't want to pry."

"…"

Himeka considered this new information. Her eyes traveled downward, and she reached for her bag.

"I see…interesting. Well, that adds up," she said, then turned away from the two. "Regardless of what that girl thinks, I've given you all the warning I can. You're the ones who choose your actions, so I can't be responsible for what happens next. I'm sorry."

"Um, you have no reason to apologize for that," Yahiro said.

She stopped walking and turned back. "It feels better to hear that from you, but I'll repeat myself one last time… Don't get involved with the Headless Rider. If you really want to fulfill your goal, you'd do better to find Shizuo Heiwajima instead."

And what she said next sent a nasty sweat trickling down Yahiro's back.

Because for the first time, her flat voice held a palpable emotion in it—thick, surging hatred.

"I think…the Headless Rider is a cruel demon."

♂♀

Outside Raira Academy

The sun had fully set outside the school.

Recruitment hours for the extracurricular clubs were over, and there were almost no students to be seen.

On trudged Yahiro and Kuon, who had just traded information.

"I dunno, what did you think? Himeka was crazy forceful back there, right? She's really hot, but I doubt any guys are gonna go after her. But that makes her all the hotter, yeah? Don't you agree?" Kuon asked.

Yahiro retorted, "I'm amazed you can talk about her like that..."

"Hey, that's my secret weapon. No matter how heavy the topic is, I'm always optimistic in an aggressive way. If Himeka's sisters turned out not to be just missing but butchered in a grisly murder scene, I'd look for the bright side. Like, hey, at least Himeka wasn't brutally slaughtered...you know?"

"That's your secret weapon? Seems more like a massive character flaw..."

Yahiro was worried that what he just said was actually tremendously cruel, but even then, he was less explicit about it than he could have been.

Kuon said, "Fair enough. Oh yeah, I can't believe you became the library committee rep."

"Huh? Why, is that bad?"

"No, not at all, not at all," Kuon reassured the panicking boy. "How did it go?"

"Well, I was telling Tatsugami before you came in that all the other people seemed nice. And the chairman was really laid-back and easy-going, too."

"Right, right, the library chairman who talked about all that stuff at orientation. Cool guy with glasses. Bet he gets all the chicks." Kuon seethed with jealousy.

"Kuon, are you joining a club or committee?"

"Me? Nah, not for me. I wanna work my job after school and do stuff like that."

"What job are you working?"

"Kind of an odd jobs gig. It's like making an allowance by running errands," Kuon said lightly, though he was clearly avoiding specifics. Yahiro decided that it was a touchy subject, perhaps, so he didn't ask a follow-up question.

Instead, he had a different question. "By the way...it seemed to me like you know about this guy named, uh...Shizuo Heiwajima."

"Know about him...? There isn't a single person who hangs out in Ikebukuro who doesn't know about that monster."

"..."

The mention of the word *monster* dug deep into Yahiro's chest.

But Kuon seemed oblivious to any changes in his companion's

demeanor. He chattered on, "Like I said yesterday, I've seen Shizuo Heiwajima throwing a vending machine...and it's crazy. I owe this third-year Kuronuma a lot, and he always tells me I should never, ever pick a fight with him."

"..."

A guy that everybody says you should never fight...

I'm jealous...

Yahiro had spent his whole life getting dragged into fights. While he savored a vision of a life of peace, Kuon blabbered on, oblivious.

"There are very few people who can actually get that guy to calm down. Apparently, he'll listen to his superior at work, but once he gets started in a fight, there's no stopping him. Not unless you're someone like Simon from the sushi place..."

He paused, then patted a fist into his palm.

"That's it, sushi! Let's go get sushi!"

"What?!"

Yahiro wasn't expecting an invitation of that sort in any way, and his cheeks twitched as he recalled the state of his wallet. "S-sorry. I don't have the cash for that..."

"What are you talking about? It's my treat! On me!"

"Whaaat?!"

Kuon smacked him on the back, but this did not placate him.

"No, I couldn't do that! I mean, sushi is expensive...even at the cheaper places with the conveyer belt..."

Even then, at a hundred yen for a little plate, that was five hundred yen for just five plates. Yahiro's family was rich, so that wasn't a large amount, but it wasn't the kind of sum you received as a gift from a classmate you met the day before. Even a favor of a hundred yen was something that Yahiro wanted to avoid if possible.

But Kuon ignored his protestations and beamed. "Actually, I like the conveyer belt stuff, but let's go get some proper sushi that gets hand delivered!"

"But...but...hang on, let me stop by the bank to withdraw some money..."

"No, it's cool, it's cool! There's a place with a special student sale for the start of the school year! There's a whole set, including some crab nigiri, for just three eighty per person!"

"Three hundred and eighty yen?!"

That was probably a small serving, like three or five pieces. If not, the low price went from being a deal to downright concerning.

Nonetheless, Kuon pulled a sales flyer out of his schoolbag and flashed it in Yahiro's face.

"It's called Russia Sushi, a place run by two Russian guys…and it's pretty famous around here."

♂♀

Apartment building near Kawagoe Highway

It was not coincidence that brought Akane Awakusu to this apartment building.

She had been escorted here before by the Headless Rider. And she'd also been here not long before that.

She remembered clearly that it was on the Kawagoe Highway. So she used one of those websites that shows the terrain as seen from the road and combed over the sites bit by bit, until at last she found a building entrance that looked distinctly familiar.

It was the day after her middle school entrance ceremony, and because the day was over just after lunch hour, Akane chose to make her way over to the apartment building where the Headless Rider lived.

"Umm…Dr. Kishitani's apartment…is…"

She remembered that the name of the doctor she met at the Headless Rider's place was Kishitani.

It was a name she'd heard on several occasions from Shizuo Heiwajima, another person Akane knew. There was no doubt he was living in the apartment with the rider.

Because it was an older building, there wasn't much of a security system presence, despite being on the pricey side. Anyone could get through the building and up to the door of the apartment.

She went up the stairs one floor at a time, checking every nameplate, until she finally arrived at a KISHITANI sign on the very top floor.

She pressed the button, but there was no reaction.

After ten seconds, she tried it again, but there was no one coming out of the apartment.

Near the door was an electricity meter, and it showed no signs of life. There probably weren't even regular appliances like a refrigerator or VCR clocks running inside.

Akane decided that they were not simply out running errands or at work. There was nothing to be done here. A steady uneasiness rose in her chest as she left the building behind.

Next, she made her way to the basement parking lot. There, too, she found only a number of cars belonging to residents of the building and no traces of the Headless Rider.

"..."

Neither was there any sign of the headless horse that once carried her here.

It was as if these things were all figments of a dream.

Suddenly plunged into deep, deep sadness, Akane could only walk around the parking lot in a daze.

It didn't need to be much. She just wanted *something* she could recognize, some bit of hope that she could still cling to.

After a fair amount of time spent doing that, she heard a familiar voice. "Miss Akane, what's the matter?"

She spun around and saw a man standing there, slightly younger than her father.

"Oh! Mr. Shiki..."

There were two other younger men with him. Their expressions were calm and pleasant, but there was an air about them that said they were not men in an ordinary line of work.

Akane knew they were from her father's organization—in other words, a group that aligned itself with certain illegal activities.

But the man named Shiki standing between them was someone she'd known since childhood, long before she was aware of what her father and grandfather did for a living. Career aside, she understood that she could trust him as a confidant of her father.

"Are you here to look for the Headless Rider, too, Mr. Shiki?" she asked.

He sighed. "I should have known you were doing much the same, miss."

"..."

"You shouldn't be getting involved in the matter of the Headless Rider. The courier is technically one of the people on *our side* of things—the people you despise so much," he said in an attempt to get her to back off.

Akane said, "But...she's not a kidnapper."

"I don't think she is, either. The problem is, if the Headless Rider is innocent, then it means that someone else we don't know is going around disappearing folks in her vicinity."

"...!"

"And you know what will happen if you happen to stumble across someone who means harm like that, don't you?" Shiki said. Akane understood that his argument was correct.

But although she recognized his point, that didn't mean she was going to back down now.

Shiki seemed to realize that as well, so he brought up a weapon he knew would have an effect. "Your father, Mikiya, was worried about you. He thinks you're going to get yourself into danger."

"...I'm fine. I'm in middle school already...," she murmured. But she couldn't hide her guilt; her eyes strayed away.

Shiki shook his head slowly. "Whether you're in middle school, or high school, or a working adult in your twenties, danger is danger. Especially when there are kidnappers making people disappear," he warned her. His tone was heavy but not intimidating. "Leave the meat to the butcher. This is a matter for us or the police."

After a long silence, Akane's head drooped.

"...All right. Please take care of the Headless Rider and her doctor."

"Of course we will."

"If we're leaving the meat to the butcher, then you won't stop me from asking around about my schoolmate at school, right? She might have only run away from home, so I want to investigate it as a runaway situation."

"Well..."

Shiki looked conflicted, but Akane persisted. "I'm not going to go anywhere dangerous. And there are other older kids who are going to look with me. I should be fine in a group, right?"

He gave her a long, piercing look, then shook his head in resignation. "Just make sure those other kids aren't going anywhere dangerous, either."

"Thank you, Mr. Shiki! I'll let you know if I learn anything!" she said, bowing her head, and turned to leave.

Once she was gone, he said to one of the younger men with him, "Escort the young lady back home."

"Yes, sir."

The young man bowed and took off running after Akane. Once she was gone from the parking lot, Shiki rotated and cracked his neck, and in a voice soft enough that the other subordinate with him couldn't hear, he muttered, "Must be the Rakuei Gym influence."

He envisioned what she'd been like in years past, and a wry grimace crossed his lips.

"Back when she was abducted, she seemed childish for her age. How much things change in just a year and a half."

♂♀

Russia Sushi

Russia Sushi was a very unconventional sushi restaurant located in the busy area of Ikebukuro.

It was off the beaten path of Sixtieth Floor Street, just near the Tokyu Hands. Because there was a bowling alley across the street, a wide clientele passed by the restaurant, from students to office workers.

The exterior was meant to look like Russia. Possibly a little *too* much like Russia. But on the inside, there was a proper counter and compartmented group tables in their own seating alcoves, just like a more conventional sushi place.

Yahiro sat at the counter, looking around the room in wonder.

It was basically like any sushi place he knew, except that all the decorations were foreign in style, and the menu was packed with items that he'd never heard of before, like Borscht Roll and Kremlin Assortment.

Between the sharp-eyed white man standing behind the counter and the huge black man serving customers, it truly felt like Yahiro and Kuon had been transported into a Japanese restaurant located somewhere in Russia instead.

"Hey, you, celebrate shining new students with good sushi. Shining you, shining sushi—eat before it become declining sushi," said the large man, whose name tag said SIMON. With his wordplay, Yahiro couldn't tell if he was really good or really bad at Japanese. He set down an assortment of pieces in front of the boys.

There were at least ten pieces of sushi there. It was hard to believe that all this was just three hundred and eighty yen per person.

Should I eat this? What if there's something weird in there…?

Yahiro was already timid by nature. He waffled awhile before reaching out with the tips of his chopsticks.

"W-well…let's try it," he said and lifted the sushi to his lips with hesitation. "It's…good," he murmured, eyes wide.

"Right? There's lots of stuff to make fun of here, but the actual taste is good."

"Yeah, it tastes great. It's like proper sushi from a restaurant in a port town."

Simon grinned at the students and gave them a vigorous thumbs-up. "Oooh, boss, you understand good. Can't fight on an empty stomach, ya? Win the battle and strap on helmet. Lose the battle, loosen your belt. Full tummy, full dreams. Taste your dreams with your favorite sushi, ya?"

He pointed at the menu up on the wall, where it said, "Cheap prices guaranteed! Everything at market price!" Yahiro decided that maybe it would be best not to order more nigiri after that.

Once he had enjoyed the entire run of sushi, he turned to Kuon again.

"Oh yeah, about that Shizuo Heiwajima guy… Where do you think I can find him?"

"Where…? If you hang out around here, you're sure to see him at least once within a three-day period. It's easy to spot him because of the blond hair and the bartender getup. More importantly, why do you want to meet him? He's dangerous, man. If you say you're just a tourist who wants to check out the local highlights, he'll kill you."

"Oh..."

"Well, they do say he's chilled out a bit recently. But like two years ago, he was savage. He would pound a street punk thirty feet through the air just for giving him a dirty look, apparently."

Overhearing their conversation, the man behind the counter spoke up as he washed his knife.

"You boys curious about Shizuo?"

"Huh? Uh...yes, sir."

"Take my advice. If you don't have anything specific to do with him, it's better for *both* sides if you leave him be," the man said, fixing them with a glare.

Unlike Simon, the restaurant owner behind the bar spoke smooth, fluent Japanese. There was a weight behind his words that forced Yahiro and Kuon to listen with their full attention.

"He's another human being like you and me. He doesn't like being gawked at as if he's some kind of zoo animal. And you don't want to get hurt for no good reason, do you?"

"Well," Yahiro started to say, but he thought better of it. Kuon looked away and shrugged.

Once again, Yahiro felt negative emotions swelling within him.

He's right, of course. I don't want to pick a fight with him...but maybe it's true that I've been thinking of this Shizuo person the same way all those people thought of me when they called me a monster. Look at what I'm doing...

What do I actually want to do *when I find Shizuo?*

The restaurant owner glanced at Yahiro's downcast face and the hands placed on the counter, then headed to his next task and continued, "From what I can see, *you fellas* have some troubles of your own you're harboring..."

"Huh?"

"Whatever it is you do, walk on the straight path. That's the key to living life without doing something you'll regret later on."

"..."

What had the man sensed in them? Yahiro felt like all the ugliness inside him was on display, and he was suddenly plunged into ice-cold fear.

"Um...thank you, sir. We'll be careful."

"..."

The man said nothing after that but resumed cutting fish in silence.

After a moment, Kuon elbowed Yahiro lightly and murmured, "There, you see? Shizuo Heiwajima's not the kind of person you get involved with out of curiosity."

"Um, right...," Yahiro mumbled lifelessly in response.

In an attempt to lift his friend's spirits again, Kuon switched topics.

"Anyway, what's up with Tatsugami's little sister? Let's think of how to search for her."

"The problem is, I don't know where to start..."

"In the past, we could have used the Dollars for this."

"Dollars?" Yahiro repeated, sipping his tea with furrowed eyebrows. He was unfamiliar with that term.

"Oh, the Dollars were a street gang that were around in Ikebukuro until two years ago. Then some stuff happened, and they broke up. They weren't really a *street* gang, though; it was mostly over the Internet... Anyone could join, from kids to office workers to housewives. It was like a club."

"Ohhh..."

Now that Kuon mentioned it, Yahiro recalled seeing a word like that while he was searching for information about the Headless Rider. He just remembered that people were talking about the group like it was a gang with hundreds of members, and he was too frightened to look into it any further.

"The thing is, the Dollars' online community was super-useful for getting info on Ikebukuro... If you wanted to find someone missing, it would pull through in a snap."

"Wow, really...? Tokyo's so amazing."

"It's not so much Tokyo as it is the Dollars being a specifically weird group. Not that the people who were in it would bother going around bragging about how they used to be Dollars." Kuon grabbed the last piece of sushi on his plate, stuffed it into his mouth, swallowed, and said mockingly, "It's behind the times, just a relic of the past leaving behind only its name and stories. Both the Dollars and the Yellow Scarves, in fact."

The smile vanished from his face, and he added one last comment, unprompted, mostly to himself.

"The Blue Squares...they've still got some life in them."

♂♀

Tokyo—abandoned building

Quite a distance away from the central parts of the metropolis, there was a particular building.

It had been abandoned in the midst of construction, by the look of it. Up to the second floor, it appeared to be an ordinary structure, but the contractors had stopped while working on the floors above it, leaving the eerie silhouette of exposed beams and metal untouched among the surroundings.

Inside the abandoned building, a man was speaking.

"Hang on... I used to be a big shot in the Blue Squares! Do you realize that? Huh?"

A man dressed like a thug with bandages over his face and arms—Horada—was taking out his anger on a bunch of kids who were far younger than he was.

"I can't believe I actually got my hopes up, hearin' the Blue Squares were back. But it's a bunch of small-time dopey kids and dumbasses."

Horada was sitting on a sofa someone must have dragged up onto the structure. Gathered across from him were members of the Blue Squares, the organization to which he had once belonged.

In the center of them was Aoba Kuronuma, who listened to Horada speak without a word.

Yoshikiri was standing nearby and sending increasingly pointed eye signals that said, *Can we kill him yet?* but Aoba sent him a single glare back to set him straight. Then he grinned and said, "Oh yes, it's quite embarrassing. The older guys have all regaled me with tales of your heroism and badassery."

"Oh? Th-they did?"

"About how you infiltrated the Yellow Scarves and totally ruined them from the inside or how you shot Shizuo Heiwajima. They all said the Blue Squares wouldn't exist today without you, Mr. Horada."

"Er...yeah! Yeah, exactly. I guess you could say it was me who kept the Blue Squares afloat at the time."

Now Yoshikiri was sending a look that said, *What does he mean, afloat?* but Aoba ignored him again.

"Yes, my brother told me all about you."

"Your brother...? Huh? You said your name was Kuronuma?"

"Yes."

"Did I know a guy named Kuronuma?" Horada wondered, opening the tab on a can of beer.

Aoba chuckled. "Oh, we have different last names because our parents divorced. In fact, I think you know my brother quite well."

"Oh yeah? What was his name?"

"His name is Ran Izumii."

Horada immediately let out his breath in the midst of taking a sip, spraying beer. "I...Izumii...?"

His face was suddenly pale, but Aoba merely smiled and pretended not to notice.

"Yes. My brother is currently a member of the Awakusu-kai. But I'm sure that he'd come right over if I let him know that you're out of jail."

"Uh-huh. Izumii, huh? Ha-ha...ha..."

Horada's attitude toward Aoba had drastically changed in the last few moments. He steadily rose from the sofa to stand. "W-well, you give my regards to Izumii. This must be difficult for a young fellow like you," he stammered, trying but failing to conceal the fear in his voice.

"Oh, yes. Libei Ying from Dragon Zombie is back, so the skirmishes never end."

Horada's shoulders twitched. "...Uh, Ying's back? You don't say."

"If you're going to back us up and be our rock, Mr. Horada, it would enable us to be bolder and really launch ourselves into this war."

"Ha...ha-ha. Shit, you know I'd love to do that. But I got stuff goin' on, yeah? And it's really not for the group's benefit if the old alum is runnin' around poppin' his mouth off and running things, right?" he said, breaking into a cold sweat as he scampered away from them. "Good luck, y'all! I'm always in your corner—you know that! Yeah? So long!"

*   *   *

And with that, he fled the building. One of Aoba's companions said, "Well, you can see why the Blue Squares fell off the map for a time."

He looked back and shrugged. "I mean, that was part of the plan from the start. I think he did a pretty good job, by his standards."

"On the other hand…even a guy in prison should know about Libei Ying. So if he's that outta the loop, he's no better than an outsider anyway."

"That's true. The current Blue Squares don't need him, I think. I was hoping that maybe he'd changed himself completely while in prison, like my brother." Aoba chuckled. He moved to sit down on the sofa where Horada had just been. "That nasty injury… That was done by Shizuo Heiwajima?"

"Yeah, he was with some of his old high school guys, picking up girls. The funny thing is, of all people, it had to be Kururi he tried to hit on."

"…"

Aoba suddenly fell silent, much to the mirth of his friends.

"Uh-oh, Aoba looks like he wants to say this isn't funny!"

"If that guy *had* tried anything on her, he'd be pulverized right about now."

"And this is the guy who says she's *not* his girlfriend. Such passion!"

"…I'll kill you!" Yoshikiri raged, reaching out to strangle Aoba, who stood up and easily sidestepped both him and the topic at hand.

"I have to say…Shizuo Heiwajima has really calmed down. Especially if *that's* all he did to the guy."

"Y-you think so…?" the others asked, skeptical.

"Look, calming down doesn't mean he can't fight anymore. But I think that since that horrible info dealer left town, his rival and all those squabbles between different groups of punks and rebels are about ready to follow his lead and vanish," Aoba said wisely, as though he weren't just a teenager in high school.

"Everything passes on to the next generation. We're no exception to the rule," he continued. A thought came to mind. He let out an exhale.

"Not that Shizuo Heiwajima has anyone ready to take on his mantle."

♂♀

Ikebukuro—several hours later

Why did things turn out this way?
Yahiro Mizuchi racked his spinning brain, trying to reflect on his past.
Images of all kinds raced through his mind, bringing back physical sensations.

Chilly air that stung the skin.
The particular smell of hot springs.
Someone holding him.
Life at the inn.   The first day of school.
The terror of being singled out by older boys.
Gushing blood, pain in his fist.
Blood   blood   blood
bloodbloodbloodbloodblood
"Monster."   "Monster."   "Monster."   "Monster."
Frightened eyes   "Monster."   Rejection   "Monster."
Broken teeth "Monster."
By the time he'd spanned from his first memories to the most recent ones, he realized that he was experiencing the sensation of his life flashing before his eyes, and his conscious mind hastily quashed those images.
No, no, no.
I need to remember…what happened one minute ago.
And…and what I should do now…
Beads of sweat hung on his cheeks. The scenery before his eyes was easy to parse.
A city intersection. A crowd of gawkers.

Standing there before him was a man with distinctive blond hair, sunglasses, and a bartender's uniform.

Shizuo Heiwajima.
The living urban legend was not a creature of online rumors and faked video footage.

He had come to stand before Yahiro in the flesh, proving the legend was real.

Fury pulsed in his temples, which was apparent even from ten feet away.

The movement of his shoulders rising and falling was like that of a wild beast.

His eyes were severe, fiercer than any mad dog with prey in sight. The average human being, if fixed with such a glare, would be frozen on the spot.

And all the hostility of this monster, Shizuo Heiwajima, was trained upon one target and one target alone: *Yahiro Mizuchi.*

Why...? Why is this happening?

The crowd around them was split.

Half of them were curious for the chance to see Shizuo Heiwajima's power for themselves.

Half of them were pitying the poor teenager who was going to die.

Almost none of their eyes were full of fear at the almighty strength of Shizuo.

Anyone who actually knew what he was capable of had already fled the scene to ensure they weren't collateral victims of a maelstrom of violence.

At the same time, the most petrified person present was Yahiro himself.

That was only natural, of course; he was under the hostile glare of a man who could pick up and hurl a vending machine one-handed.

And Yahiro was a coward by nature.

He didn't want to die. He was scared. He wanted to live.

He wanted to get away from the terror.

So his mind spun faster: How did it come to this?

Maybe then he could find the solution, the way to put distance between himself and the terror.

* * *

I was talking about this person at the sushi restaurant...
Then the chef there told me not to look for him...
Then we went around looking for Tatsugami's little sister...
Oh, that's right. It was a coincidence.
I got dragged into this through no fault of my own.

It felt like quite a long time had passed, but it was really only a matter of seconds.

Perhaps the endorphins rushing through his brain along with the memories of his life had thrown off his sense of time. But illusion or not, the span was enough for Yahiro to finally remember what happened a minute before.

And then again, he understood—that the aggression directed at him was caused by his own cowardice.

Yahiro steadied his gaze, it following down Shizuo Heiwajima's side to the ground.

Lying on the asphalt, faceup, was a green-haired boy.

Yahiro got spooked—that was all.

Spooked that the very first "friend" he'd made in his life might be lost right before his eyes.

Spooked that doing nothing might mean the death of Kuon Kotonami.

He just wanted to run away.

♂♀

A few minutes earlier

Shizuo Heiwajima was in a foul mood that day.

When he popped his head into the office, they were talking about an odd story.

"The Headless Rider is kidnapping people."

The new employee there had no idea that Shizuo and the Headless Rider were acquaintances. He was smugly passing off info he'd read from a news site that accumulated Ikebukuro information from affiliate blogs.

Because the site made its money off the ad banners around each news article, they were incentivized to put flashy, attention-grabbing titles on their articles to get people to click on them.

Shizuo happened to see the title on the article that was open on the new employee's tablet: *[Urban Legend Resumes] Turns out the serial disappearances in Ikebukuro are being done by the Headless Rider!*

When he demanded to know, "Where can I go to find the piece of shit who wrote this article?" it scared everyone else out of the room until the company president and Tom arrived at the office.

Without anyone to unleash his anger upon, Shizuo had no choice but to hold down that rage in the pit of his stomach for the rest of the day's work.

"C'mon...don't be so prickly, man. Let's eat some sushi and forget about our troubles."

"...Yessir."

"I'm pretty sure Russia Sushi's running some specials in addition to their new student deal."

Shizuo had finished the day safely, despite his foul mood. He followed Tom to Russia Sushi. But the block of entertainment venues across the street from Russia Sushi, such as the bowling alley, had a number of people lingering outside.

"You know what? I think it's basically undeniable that the Headless Rider is a kidnapper," said a green-haired boy loudly, as he bought a beverage from the line of vending machines along the wall.

"What's this all about?"

Yahiro had been walking around the area, hoping to find information about their missing target. They did not get any useful information from Kuon's circle of friends and had come back to Russia Sushi. They stopped to grab drinks from a vending machine when Kuon brought up the topic of the Headless Rider.

"Well, I mean...her name was Akane, right? I know we told Akane that if there's a misunderstanding, it's important to clear it up...but at the end of the day, the Headless Rider's a monster, ya know?"

"Er, well..."

"And you came all the way to Ikebukuro to see a monster, didn't you?"

"Well...umm...," murmured Yahiro, unable to answer firmly. He hit the button on the machine.

"And even before that, whether the rider's human or monster, they're clearly up to no good. There's no surprise if that guy's kidnapping people. I was posting about that on Twittia, and nobody even argued with me. Everyone knows it's true, deep down. The Headless Rider's a scumbag who would totally kidnap people."

"Twittia?"

"Uh...it's kind of like a blog. Oh yeah, and my twits got picked up in a bunch of news articles. It was pretty hilarious. Though I feel bad for that little Akane girl."

"They got put in a news article? Do you get...some kind of reward or payment for that?"

Yahiro had only used the Internet for looking up info about the Headless Rider and similar topics, so he did not understand the finer workings of social networks and news aggregators. Sometimes Kuon's Internet discussions left him behind.

He crouched and grabbed the can from the bottom tray of the machine, waiting for the answer to his question.

"..."

"?"

No answer was forthcoming.

"Kuon?"

Yahiro stood up and turned around, assuming his friend hadn't heard him—and saw what had happened.

A man with blond hair, temples twitching, had Kuon by the collar of his shirt and was lifting him off the ground.

For an instant, Yahiro froze, not understanding what had happened.

Once he realized the man was Shizuo Heiwajima, a plethora of questions exploded in his mind.

Huh?

Shizuo Heiwajima...?

I saw him in a video.

The real thing?

He's lifting Kuon with one hand...

Wait, but—why?

He couldn't move from the spot. It was like a bad dream—but Kuon's gurgling brought him back to his senses.

"H-hey! What are you doing?!" he cried, trying to rush over, but a man with dreadlocks intercepted him.

"Hang on. Keep your distance; you don't want to get hurt."

"..."

The man didn't seem to be hostile. He spoke to the blond man with concern on his features. "Hey, Shizuo..."

But the words didn't reach Shizuo Heiwajima. His forehead pulsing, he grunted, "Hey...boy... Was it you? Are you the one who's been spreading bullshit rumors...?"

"Aagh...stop...help..." Kuon gasped, kicking his legs helplessly. "I didn't say anything about you, Mr. Heiwajima! It's true! P-please believe me!"

"What...? I don't care about me... I know I've earned me whatever people want to say about me after the way I've lived my life," Shizuo growled, barely in control, his voice like a curse from the depths of hell. "But if you treat my friend...like some kind of kidnapper...you don't expect me to let that pass, do you...?"

"F-friend...? Then you mean...you're really friends with the Headless Rider...?"

"She ain't the kind of person who abducts people and brings sorrow to the world... I mean, she might drive that bike without lights on...so I guess you could knock her for that, but..."

He was clearly doing his best to keep himself from punching Kuon, despite his fury.

"And on top of that, you're sayin' you lied to Akane...? Well, that just ain't right now, is it...? Huh...?"

At this point, Yahiro understood Shizuo Heiwajima's rage. It was quite simple.

His friend was being treated like a kidnapper, and it made sense that he was angry about someone spreading that rumor to the public at large.

And from his own words, it seemed that Shizuo Heiwajima knew Akane Awakusu as well.

A number of different factors were intertwined in this situation, so it was no surprise that Shizuo Heiwajima was furious.

This timing couldn't be worse...! And Kuon just had to do what was guaranteed to set him off...

...?

Something else shivered through his chest. Something that was not fear of Shizuo.

It was the strange, hinky feeling he'd felt about Kuon earlier, but Yahiro was not in any state to explore that now.

As for Kuon, he was jabbering away, pleading his case. "N-no, wait, please, sir... I wasn't the one who came up with this idea that the Headless Rider is kidnapping people... *Koff...*"

"Hey, kid. I know it's not fair, but take my advice and apologize to him. Okay?" said the other man to the boy in Shizuo's grip.

But Kuon was too panicked to hear him or understand. In fact, he promptly made the situation markedly worse.

"Let's just chill out, okay? Okay?! P-plus, you know that if something happens to me, it'll be bad for your *brother*, right?"

"..."

"I know about you. Your brother's a superstar, right? If I tell people about this online, they'll totally flame his blog and everything! You want that?" he said, a threat as much as it was a plea.

The man in the dreads suddenly went pale. He'd already seen what happened earlier to a guy drowning in debt who tried the same threats.

"No, you idiot! Are you trying to get yourself killed?!"

"Huh...?" Kuon gaped. "Wha...?"

Then he realized that his body was suddenly free-floating in air.

"Huh... Wha...? Whoaaaa?!"

And as he fell, Shizuo's fist thrust upward toward him.

There was a *krak*, more of a bursting noise than a thudding impact.

People turned around in reaction and saw a green-haired boy fly through the air.

Kuon hurtled several yards, then rolled and tumbled on the asphalt.

"Aaah! K-Kuon! Wha...?!"

Yahiro tried to rush toward his friend but stumbled along the way. That was when he realized that his legs were quaking.

Wh-what...? What's going on...? I've never felt like this before.

Ever since childhood, Yahiro had lived in fear of many things. But the "fear" he felt toward Shizuo Heiwajima in this moment was unlike anything he'd ever experienced. It was a new sensation to him.

"Well, great... Ya did it now." Tom grimaced, shaking his head.

He should probably call for an ambulance. For now, he was going to check on the boy to see if he was all right, but then he noticed something.

"…Shizuo?"

Shizuo was quickly striding toward the fallen youth. Tom figured he felt bad that he'd gone overboard and was about to help him up.

However, that optimistic thought left Tom's mind as soon as it entered. Rage clearly painted Shizuo's face as he walked past.

Wait, are you kidding? If you hit him while he's down, the kid really is gonna die!

"Hey! Wait, Shizuo!"

Tom's usual course of action was to stand back and wait for the storm to pass when Shizuo flew into one of his rages, but this time he had to intercede.

Shizuo did not stop, however. He didn't seem to hear a word.

The man in the bartender uniform reached the green-haired boy on the ground and lifted back one of his legs.

What?! Is he gonna kick him?!

"Shizuo!"

Tom rushed forward to protect the boy.

And something passed by the side of Tom's head with tremendous force.

"?!"

Stunned by the whipcrack of air being split by his ear, Tom saw the object slam into the back of Shizuo's head.

It all happened so fast.

There was a hard, heavy smack, and a second later, the object fell to the ground.

The projectile was an aluminum drink can, rattling heavily over the asphalt. It had flown past at blinding speed, struck the back of Shizuo's head, then fallen to the ground from the effect of gravity.

That was a simple enough action to describe, but everyone who witnessed it held their breath, anticipating the eruption that was about to unfold.

The can was full of liquid and hurled with the force of a baseball. That made it a dangerous weapon and possibly even fatal if it struck someone's head the wrong way.

Shizuo stopped before he kicked Kuon and slowly turned around, creaking like a spring-wound toy.

When he finished, he was looking at a boy.

Like the green-haired one at his feet, this boy was wearing a Raira Academy uniform.

His shoulders were heaving up and down, and a cold sweat was running down his face. He was frozen in the position of someone having thrown an object, which made it very clear that he was the one who had hurled the unopened can at Shizuo.

Even still, Shizuo glanced at the can at his feet, opened his mouth, and—to confirm—asked, "Was it you...who just threw that...at me...?"

His voice came from the very bowels of hell.

Beads of sweat hung on the boy's forehead. His breathing was heavy. To all eyes, he seemed about ready to pass out in sheer fright.

But the boy swallowed hard and, in a trembling voice, said, "Y-you're...going too far."

Then he straightened up and delivered an ultimatum to the monster standing just a few yards away.

"If you want a fight...I'll give you one."

♂♀

And that was what led to this moment.

Oh, right.

Yahiro vividly recalled the reason he was in this situation now, soaking in absolute fury and ill will.

I picked a fight.

...Wait, I did? Are you kidding?

He was always the one who was getting forced into fights. He was always the one terrified of it happening. What was he doing?

The presence of this question made Yahiro fear *himself*.

He was being crushed, clamped between the fear of the deadly man before him and the distrust of his own decision-making.

His classmate Kuon had been attacked by Shizuo Heiwajima, the monster. And in witnessing that, Yahiro's greatest fear was losing someone forever—a person who would actually laugh and be friends with a guy like him.

He would have probably done the same thing if it were Himeka on the ground at Shizuo's feet.

Although it was unlikely to ever happen, Yahiro might have picked the same fight even if it were Akane Awakusu, Mairu Orihara, or the library committee chairman he'd just met earlier today.

He understood this action endangered his life.

But the fear even outweighed that. The fear that, despite the life he'd led to this point, he would turn and flee to save his own skin, abandoning the first people to ever treat him like a fellow human being.

In other words, he wasn't summoning his courage or unleashing a noble act of sacrifice.

It wasn't reason. It was instinct.

His instinct to run from fear had chosen his action for him.

It had chosen the madness of stopping Shizuo Heiwajima.

"…I'll ask one more question," said Shizuo, slowly inclining his body toward Yahiro. "Do you also think Ce…er…the Headless Rider is a kidnapper?"

"…"

His answer would determine his fate—that was clear to Yahiro. He chose honestly.

"…I don't know. I've never met the Headless Rider."

"Earlier you were saying something about coming to 'see a monster'… Is that what you think of the Headless Rider…? Huh?"

If he were crafty enough to simply lie about this, he would have been able to avoid his fears in other ways. He would not have been called a monster.

Here, Yahiro's sense of reason kicked in.

Kuon was still lying on the ground at Shizuo's feet.

That meant all Shizuo Heiwajima's hostility *must be* pointed at *him* now.

That was the decision of Yahiro's reason.

His instinct had chosen to pick a fight with another person for the first time in his life—and his reason led him to issue a challenge for the first time in his life.

Remember, remember.

Out of all the books and TV shows he'd absorbed in his life, he tried to recall the right line of dialogue to say in this situation and use it.

"Yeah, that's right," Yahiro said, clenching his fists and glaring at Shizuo as hard as he could. "I came here to Ikebukuro…to check out monsters like you and the Headless Rider."

Despite marshaling the full memory banks of his past, the best Yahiro could do was repeat the information back at Shizuo.

But it was enough to bring the full, undivided focus of Shizuo Heiwajima to bear on himself.

"I see… Well, that settles that, then…"

Shizuo began to walk toward him, and once he was standing before Yahiro, he clenched his fist.

"If you're checkin' monsters out when they're not in cages…then you can't complain if the monster…beats you to deaaaaaaath!" he roared, a wild beast echoing between the parallel buildings of Ikebukuro.

Wreathed in the air pressure of a ballistic missile, Shizuo's fist rocketed toward Yahiro's face—and the boy from Akita experienced the greatest fear he'd ever felt in his life.

♂♀

Tokyo—Yahiro's apartment building

"Whoa, what happened to your face?" asked Saburo, the younger brother of the building landlord, when Yahiro returned home.

Saburo was not like Jirou at all. He was more of a free spirit, whose life mostly consisted of a singer named Ruri Hijiribe and his van.

He spotted Yahiro while he was waxing the van in the yard of his home next to the apartment building.

"Uh…I fell down the stairs."

"Oh, come on—try something a little more convincing," Saburo said, eyeing the numerous bruises and scrapes on Yahiro's face, some of which were swelling.

His clothes were fairly ragged, too. Clearly, he had not suffered this kind of damage from an ill-fated encounter with some stairs.

"What happened? Hey, is someone messing with you? I'm not gonna step in and get involved in any old argument between kids, but if

they're ganging up on you, that's another story. I can't just stand back and watch as a relative gets beaten bloody."

"Er, no..."

Realizing that further lying was only going to make the situation worse, Yahiro decided on honesty.

"It wasn't a gang up... It was a one-on-one fight. I'm sorry," he said, bowing.

Saburo just smiled. "You don't have to apologize to me. When I was your age, I was fighting all the time. As long as you're not picking on anyone or stealing their lunch money, I'm not gonna chew you out. But I can tell my brother that you fell down the stairs."

"...Thank you."

"Boy, they really got you good, huh? Who were you fighting? Is there a real feisty brawler at Raira now? Or was it someone from Kushinada High?" Saburo asked casually, returning to the waxing of his car.

"Um...I don't know if you know him or not, but he wears a bartender's outfit, and his name is Heiwajima," Yahiro answered. The wax squeaked as Saburo's hand froze.

He looked back, his brows knitted with disbelief.

"You...what? Seriously? Why?"

"Oh, um... I accidentally got him mad... It was my fault."

"Wait a second—are you okay?! Do you need to visit the hospital?"

"I'll be all right... After he knocked me out, he was nice enough not to keep going."

Unaware of what was going through his relative's mind, Saburo exhaled with relief. "Well, that's good to hear. I guess it really is true that Heiwajima's chilled out these days..."

"So you know him?"

"Yeah. A bit. In the old days, you wouldn't get off that easy from Shizuo Heiwajima. He would have put you in the hospital."

"Oh, I see..."

Togusa returned to waxing the car. Over his shoulder, he said, "Well, he doesn't tend to hold on to grudges against ordinary folks. If you ever run into him again, just make sure you give him a proper apology for ticking him off, and he won't pick on you after that."

"I see... Thank you for the advice."

Yahiro bowed to him and returned to his room.

After he left, Togusa continued waxing and muttered to himself, "That's weird… For a run-in with Shizuo, he sure seemed to be in a good mood.

"Hopefully he didn't get hit so hard that a few screws got knocked loose."

♂♀

Yahiro's room

Back in his apartment room, Yahiro exhaled heavily and fell onto the floor.

He lay there, his back on the ground, staring at the ceiling.

"…I lost."

He lost.

Speaking it out loud, making it official, brought a swirl of conflicting emotions to his chest.

"For the first time in my life…I lost a fight…"

All the bones in his body creaked. Pain seared his flesh.

He did not know how to resolve the mixture of physical pain and emotion racking his being. He just lay there, staring in a daze.

After ten minutes, Yahiro murmured, "It feels bad. But it feels good. What is this?"

Shizuo Heiwajima was truly powerful. He couldn't deny the shock that someone like him was actually real.

He was reminded of the words of the traveler, who had told him, "You're a normal person."

"I guess…I'm normal after all…"

Never in his wildest dreams had he imagined that he would feel bad about losing a fight. But at the same time, he was overjoyed that he felt that way.

"I guess…I can be human after all."

Even the pain ringing through his body felt comfortable. It told him he really was human.

"Or else…I guess it might mean that both me and Mr. Heiwajima are monsters."

In either case, Yahiro felt salvation.

He wasn't alone.

Life was more than a cage of tedium and fatigue.

Learning that fact alone made life worth living now.

Also…I'm glad that Kuon didn't die.

Kuon had been all right in the end. After Shizuo Heiwajima left, he'd gotten up and helped Yahiro to his feet.

They stumbled back in a daze, barely sharing a word, but all Yahiro could feel now was gratefulness that they were both alive.

He thought about the first friend he'd ever made and about what Himeka might say about his injuries tomorrow, as sleep eventually overtook him.

Lastly, he envisioned the faces of all the people he'd met over the last few days and mumbled to himself as he smiled with satisfaction and drifted off.

"I feel like maybe…I can make it here…"

♂♀

The problem was, Yahiro was still missing part of the picture.

He hadn't yet realized what he'd done.

♂♀

Rooftop—night

"Yo. There you are."

Tom opened the door to the roof and spotted Shizuo looking the other way.

They were on top of their company building, where anyone in the office could go up onto the roof. They had finished their report on the day's work, and Shizuo was now watching the city below.

"You still bothered by what happened?"

"…You could say that."

"About the black-haired kid, right?"

"Yeah... Now I'm realizing that maybe he wasn't such a bad guy...," Shizuo murmured.

Tom shrugged and said, "Seems like he chose to challenge you so he could save that kid with the green hair."

"You think so, too, Tom?" Shizuo said, still turned away to watch the night scenery. "I gotta apologize to him the next time I see him..."

"Look, it's not worth feeling that bad about, is it? Throwing a full can at your head while you weren't looking is the sort of thing that could kill a normal person. Maybe he feels like he owes you an apology, too."

"..."

"But more than that, I'm just amazed," Tom said, lining up next to Shizuo to survey the view. "The world's bigger than you think."

"...Sure is."

"You did win in the end, but..."

Tom glanced over at Shizuo's face—and the cracked sunglasses and bruises and scrapes beneath them.

"That was the first time I've ever seen you get hit that many times and thrown to the ground in a good old-fashioned fistfight... Though I did see your arm get dislocated that one time before."

Shizuo's arm was held in a sling wrapped around his neck. Tom glanced at the battered sight of him, then envisioned the face of the boy who'd fought Shizuo like an equal and felt a cold sweat break out.

"Go figure there's a high schooler *that* strong out there..."

INTERMISSION
Online Rumors (3)

On the Ikebukuro information site IkeNew! Version I.KEBU.KUR.O

```
Popular Post: [Seeking Information] Supposedly
there's a high schooler who can go toe to toe
with Shizuo Heiwajima!
```

Greetings. Your site administrator, this is.
Received some news today that is rather difficult to believe, I have.
The infamous Shizuo Heiwajima had a fight with a teenage boy and very nearly lost, he did.

(Abridged)
See this video for reference → *[External link]*

It's just cell phone footage from a distance, so you can't see faces too well, but clearly wearing a Raira Academy uniform, the other combatant is.

And most certainly putting up a good fight against Shizuo Heiwajima, he is.

We haven't heard any stories about Raira having such a powerhouse last year, so most likely a new student, this boy is.

...But wait a moment. A boy around fifteen years old, holding his own against Shizuo?

Uncertain, too much of our information is.

If anyone can give us a more detailed profile of this boy, please use the e-mail form to drop a line to the admin, I ask.

The Ikebukuro of tomorrow depends on you.

Incidentally, intensely unpopular this type of writing has been. But continue all month, it will.

Continue, it will.

♂♀

A selection of ordinary twits from the social network Twittia

Shizuo Heiwajima got beat? For real?

→He didn't get beat. He won in the end.

→For real? Somebody lied.

→But he did get knocked down a couple times.

→For real?

I heard Shizuo had beef with a high school kid. Did he throw a machine?

→He tried to, but the kid got in his wheelhouse and kicked his knee first.

→OW holy shit!

→What do you mean?

→Normally your knee would shatter if someone kicked it while you're lifting a vending machine.

→Normally you wouldn't lift a vending machine at all...

Damn, Raira is crazy.

→ Isn't Kushinada High more dangerous around that area?

→ Kushinada's old news.

What's up with the admin of IkeNew talking like he's Yoda or something? Does he have no sense of shame?

→ Really? You're bringing that up now?

→ I mean, how old is that guy?

→ No idea. He never puts up any pictures of his face.

→ I think he should talk in cat puns.

→ No idea what you're talking ameowt

CHAPTER 4

CHAPTER 4 A
The Newcomer

Ikebukuro–several years ago

"So you want to know about the Headless Rider?" asked the info broker, dressed in a black coat with a fur fringe. He shrugged his shoulders.

His client asked how much it would cost.

"The price is the same as for any other information. But what I can tell you is more limited than most topics. For one thing, the Headless Rider is one of my sources."

He leaned back into his office chair and stared up at the ceiling.

"First of all, I want to make one thing clear. The Headless Rider is literally headless. Not a trick, not a costume. We're talking about an actual monster. Or spook; or goblin; or phantom, fairy, freak, ghosty, creature, urban legend, cryptid... People are free to use whatever word they want, and I have no interest in debating specific definitions."

Once satisfied that the client wasn't angry or mocking in the wake of that declaration of the Headless Rider's inhuman nature, he smirked and continued.

"Ah yes, so you've seen your share of the rider, then. You can't see such a creature in person and still think it belongs to this world. I mean, if you saw that silent motorcycle and the shadow that exudes from the rider's body, you'd have to be quite eccentric to think that was humanly possible. Then again, the pace of human progress is always beyond what you think. Perhaps modern technology can do that now."

Then he diverted the topic slightly.

"Human possibilities are truly incredible, don't you agree? They say that anything mankind can envision will be achieved. When neuroscience and virtual reality develop further, we'll be unable to tell the difference between dreams and the future anymore. The time lag between 'now' and 'later' will cease to exist. The moment you dream of flying, a device will capture that thought and send the image of flight directly to your brain, perhaps. Or maybe humanity will fall idle and cease to advance. I accept the future in either case."

He looked down from the ceiling and faced his guest, beaming happily.

"I love humanity, you see," he said, bringing the detoured topic back to the main road. "Or to flip it around, I do not love anything that isn't humanity. You might even say I hate it. But at least for the moment, I don't hold any particular loathing or hostility for the Headless Rider."

His mouth curled upward, and his eyes sparkled.

"But I say 'for the moment' because...if she tried to change human society itself, I'm certain I would hate her for that."

Then he looked away, reflecting on the topic of the Headless Rider.

"The Headless Rider learned how to be a person by living among them. She's a monster that wound up blending into human society for reasons of her own, learning what's important and what is forbidden. Ironically, because of that, she's actually got more morals than your average hoodlum. In fact, it's startling just how rapidly she managed to mimic humans."

He paused there and stared right into his client's eyes, his mouth twisted in a grimace.

"But of course, no human being is going to view the Headless Rider as another human. A vampire is one thing—it might as well be a person with a bad dental history. But she's missing something that is extremely important for a human being to have: a head."

The client asked what he was trying to say.

"What do human beings do when they see something alien?"

He stood up from his chair and walked over to a bookshelf full of a variety of titles.

"They revere it, they tremble in fear, they view it as an escape from dreary reality. Or they try to use it, or try to kill it, or try to purge it from their sight—or simply run away... What will you do? Not that I'm particularly hung up on the answer." The info broker traced a spin with his finger and repeated to his client, "I love human beings."

Then he seemed to remember something.

"Well, I do happen to know one person, a real eccentric, who said he loved the Headless Rider as a woman. But I can respect even that choice because it's a choice made by a human."

He pulled out a number of books and began to organize them.

"Human beings exhibit a variety of reactions in the face of the alien. Even if it occurs not in a monster but in another human. Mighty warriors are hailed as heroes in wartime, but when peace returns, they are feared as monsters for their extreme strength. It's only natural that reactions change depending on the individual, the time, and the society."

The info dealer's shoulders rose, and his voice dripped with irony.

"In that sense, when a monster is living in the midst of society, what's important is not on the human side. It's on the monster's side.

"Out of all the many, many reactions that humanity gives you, whose hand will you take?"

♂♀

Ikebukuro—present day

"A high schooler...who can fight on equal terms with Shizuo Heiwajima?"

Aoba's voice was full of naked skepticism and honest surprise, as if to say it would be incredible if it were true.

They were in the busy part of Ikebukuro, and the clock would soon be hitting midnight.

While the crowd had died down, the place was still busy, just full of a different clientele, like office workers on their way home from drinking.

After Horada left, Aoba and his friends went back into the busy part of the city to hang out.

Mairu had sent him a message saying, *"We're looking for a girl named Ai Tatsugami. Ask Kuon for the details!"* but Kuon hadn't shown up for the Blue Squares hangout, so there was nothing to do on that end.

I'll have to ask Mairu or Kururi at school tomorrow, Aoba decided. In the air around him were the buzzing rumors.

"I heard Shizuo Heiwajima was in bad shape."

"Yeah, like he almost lost the fight?"

It sounded preposterous to Aoba, but he couldn't help his curiosity, and when they stopped at a nearby corner, he whipped out his smartphone to check.

He soon found the information he was looking for, between a number of news sites and social media feeds.

"Oh, shit, it's *IkeNew!*"

There was an article right on the familiar Ikebukuro news site, but Aoba still couldn't be sure of what he was reading—until he finally saw the video.

This…isn't…special effects.

Is Shizuo Heiwajima going easy on him? No, that's not it.

In fact…how is he moving like that…?

The boy in the Raira Academy uniform was weaving away from Shizuo's fists with inhuman footwork and striking back quickly and accurately.

Aoba was shocked to learn that there was a student at his school who could move like this, but there was something else in the video that caught his attention.

The quality of the video was poor, and it seemed to have been taken from a distance on maximum zoom.

He couldn't make out the face of the combatant fighting Shizuo—but he had a very clear look at a person nearby, who slowly got to his feet.

It was another male wearing the Raira uniform. With green hair.

"Kotonami…"

Caught right in the same frame with the boy who was fighting toe to toe with Shizuo was Aoba's underclassman and fellow Blue Square.

Understanding came to his mind, along with a number of emotions. Aoba grinned.

*   *   *

"Who the hell did he find…? *What* the hell did he find?"

♂♀

Tokyo—abandoned factory

"You think Shizuo Heiwajima was, like…sick or something? Maybe he had the flu."

The voice echoed through the unused factory building.

This building had previously been used as a secret hideout of sorts by both the Yellow Scarves and Blue Squares over the years. Now that the Yellow Scarves were gone and the Blue Squares had moved elsewhere, a new gang ruled this turf.

Dragon Zombie.

The motorcycle gang had made their home around Ikebukuro for ages. Before the era of color-repping street gangs arrived, they had been one of the two most feared groups in the city, the other being their rival, Jan-Jaka-Jan.

But as the times changed, so did the idea of the youth subculture custom motorcycle gang, the *bosozoku*. Jan-Jaka-Jan was now an underground group, working as a street-level arm of the Awakusu-kai. And because of the circumstances that took their leader, Libei Ying, away from Ikebukuro, Dragon Zombie had become a gang with name value only and little substance.

The remaining members did what they could to keep the group going, taking jobs for an info broker—but when that broker skipped town, it seemed that the writing was on the wall for the gang.

However, that just set up a new turning point.

Their leader came home.

"Shizuo's such a monster. That's never changed," said a man in his early twenties. He had his back to the rest of the group inside the factory, his eyes trained up near the ceiling.

That was only natural, because their leader, Libei Ying, was engaged in a very different activity while he spoke to his followers.

His hands were nimbly moving back and forth, hurling a multitude of objects into the air for the other hand to catch. He was juggling.

Normally, you would assume he was half-joking around while holding that conversation, but not a single person around him was laughing or even smiling.

The objects he was juggling were wide-bladed Chinese weapons called *liuyedao*, or "willow-leaf sabers." Many people in Japan thought of this weapon as a Blue Dragon Sword, but that was a misconception; that name actually corresponded to a long-handled, bladed spear.

In any case, they were vicious-looking weapons. The ceiling light reflected off naked edges as they spun and danced right over Libei's head.

Two young women were sitting on oil drums resting on either side of Libei. They must have trusted his skill implicitly, because they showed no concern over the fact that they could easily be sliced by the flying weapons with one wrong move.

They each gave their own commentary.

"We happened to be there when they were fighting."

"It was really amazing. He was just like Shizuo."

The juggling man smiled, delighted by what he was hearing. He said to all the cohorts standing behind him, "How curious. I bet this will lead to something fun."

Then he changed up the movement of his hands, and as though wrapping them up in his arms, he caught multiple swords out of the air at once.

When he had them all in his control, he spun around and spread his hands in a dramatic fashion.

"I'd really like to meet this boy."

♂♀

Tokyo—back alley

"S-some guy was throwing fists with Shizuo like it was nothing?! Are you serious?!" Horada cried, dropping the can of beer and rushing over to the other hoodlums. "You better be! I don't want to find out you're bullshittin' me!"

"N-no, I'm serious! I was there when it happened! I couldn't really see his face 'cause it was far away, but I'm sure the guy was a student at Raira Academy!"

Horada clenched a fist without realizing it. "That's crazy... You know Shizuo—that guy's a total monster! If there's a kid on his level out there, we *gotta* get him in with us... You know it!"

"You serious?"

"Then I can go back and talk shit to those kids in the Blue Squares. I could even mess with Dragon Zombie! I'll rule Ikebukuro again!"

Had Horada ever ruled Ikebukuro in the first place? His friends tried to think of when that would have been, but nobody wanted to question him out loud.

After all, they all agreed that having a powerful pawn at their disposal would dramatically change their status around town.

♂♀

A rooftop in Ikebukuro

Once he'd gotten a good dose of the night breeze, Tom admonished his coworker.

"Look...you went a bit too far tonight, Shizuo. The kid was knocked out cold, and you went after him for another kick? That's not you."

Shizuo looked conflicted. "Yeah...I'm sorry. But the thing is, that kid with the green hair... He was mostly unharmed."

"Huh? What do you mean? He wouldn't be fine if you hit him..."

"The moment I hit him, he caught the punch with both hands. And he used that leverage to push himself off my fist."

"..."

Tom was well aware that Shizuo was not the kind of person who made weak excuses.

And he also noticed that Shizuo was smoldering with a particular anger—something he was holding deep in his gut, away from the surface.

"I get the feeling...I mighta been screwed over back there.

*   *   *

"That green-haired kid… He's no different from that *fleabrain*."

♂♀

Takadanobaba—Kuon's apartment

"I—I did it just like you said, okay? I started talking about the rumors in the office this morning, right around Shizuo Heiwajima… Honestly, I thought he was gonna kill me. This job wasn't worth it. You owe me hazard pay or something…"

Kuon smirked as the young man on the other end of the phone pleaded.

"Now, now, let's not get greedy. You know I could tell Shizuo the truth, right? That the new guy at work was spreading stories about the Headless Rider to make him mad, all in the hope of scrounging up a little money…"

"…N-no…Please! Anything but that! I won't ask for money again, okay? Okay?!"

After their conversation finished, Kuon placed another call to a different person. He walked around his apartment, humming as it connected. He did not appear to be particularly hurt after his encounter earlier.

"Hey…sorry about that. The guy I hired started getting greedy with me."

"＿＿"

"Yeah… This was really startling. I wasn't expecting it," Kuon admitted, sitting down on the sofa with his smartphone to his ear. "I was thinking I'd get my ass kicked so bad by Shizuo Heiwajima that he'd go to jail for good this time."

"＿＿? ＿＿. ＿＿!"

"…Nah, the people in town are tired of getting served Shizuo. So you gotta take him off the menu for a while. By the time he gets out of prison, he's fresh again, see?"

It was a strange thing to say. He wore a very odd, unboyish smile full of patronizing smugness.

*   *   *

"It's time for a new star to take the stage. And I wanna make sure there's plenty of advertising."

♂♀

"A guy on Shizuo's level?!"

"Then he's invincible to everyone but Shizuo!"

"What middle school was he from?!"

"I dunno, actually."

"Is there a higher-res video out there?!"

"Is he actually tougher than Shizuo?"

"Never heard of him around here."

"An outsider, then?"   "Find him."   "Find him."   "Whatever it takes to find him!"

In the span of a single night, the story raced all through Ikebukuro. He hadn't beaten Shizuo Heiwajima. He'd just put up a good fight. But that alone was an abnormal event.

There was one man who had fought Shizuo with knives and vehicles. However, it was simply unheard of for someone to hurt Shizuo with their bare hands. Sometimes people talked about Simon from the sushi shop, but he helped bring Shizuo back to reason when he was in a rage and had never actually fought him, so no one knew for certain who'd win.

Because nearly everyone reacted to the news the same way, it set off a shock wave through the city—and drew great interest from the public.

Shizuo Heiwajima had become a household name among the young people of Ikebukuro.

And anyone who was his equal in combat became news by that fact alone.

As for Yahiro Mizuchi himself, he was peacefully sleeping, completely unaware of what was happening elsewhere.

In the depths of his sleep, he dreamed.

He was leading a normal life with many others.

In this dream, he enjoyed the world that general society considered to be "ordinary."

This was his hope for the future.

He would surely forget what it was about after he woke up, but it was a hope that he would continue to hold in his waking life.

He had no idea that he was rapidly becoming a new urban legend.

The latest urban legend had no idea he was breathing new life into the city of Ikebukuro. He was fast asleep.

Peacefully counting sheep.

CHAPTER 4 B
The Returnee

An excerpt from Shinichi Tsukumoya's closed blog

Hi, it's been a while since my last update.

My friend the info dealer has vanished from the city, and I haven't had much to do lately.

The Dollars are gone, too; plus, the Headless Rider hasn't been seen in half a year.

If you're still coming to this page, it's probably because you want to know about the string of disappearances lately.

Before I talk about that, I should say something about the protagonist of this case.

Yes, the protagonist.

If you were to describe a life as a story, in most cases, you would pin the label of *protagonist* on the person whose story is being told.

However, in circumstances where the ties that bind people are complex and intertwined—such as an incident like this—viewing the situation in an objective manner will sometimes require making a protagonist out of several people.

The case of the serial disappearances in Ikebukuro is no exception to this.

The protagonist role shifts depending on the direction of your objectivity—the side committing the incident or the side pursuing the truth. The observer's personal interests will also have a large effect on the narrative lens.

In my personal lens, the Headless Rider is the protagonist.

Yes, despite having vanished half a year ago, the rider is the protagonist of the story about the past month's disappearances.

You might find that strange…and yet, despite her absence from Ikebukuro, she is treated as a central figure in the incident, isn't she?

We also have that cliché…that the hero shows up at the last minute.

But if you view this incident with the Headless Rider as the protagonist—well, what a foolish and unimpressive protagonist she makes.

After all, she has no idea of the disaster befalling her. She won't know until the event grows so large that it is nearly out of anyone's control.

♂♀

Kawagoe Highway—outside a convenience store late at night

It was after two in the morning.

A man exited the convenience store and found a shadow blocking his path.

A literal shadow.

The figure was covered in an all-black riding suit, like a black outfit with no logos or patterns. It was as if it had been dipped in the blackest ink imaginable, so black that it seemed to absorb all the light coming from the store. It was darker than the night around it.

However, the shadow was also wearing a flashy Hawaiian shirt and a lei of flowers on top of the suit.

The especially strange part about this shadow was above the neck. The figure was wearing a helmet with an odd design on it. While the neck and everything below it might have been completely black, the helmet and its design were an artistic contrast.

The face cover on the helmet was as black as the tinted glass on a luxury automobile. It reflected only the neon light of the convenience store and did not offer any glimpse into what was behind it.

In total contrast, the helmet was also decorated with stickers of various cute and minimalistic mascot characters from different regions of the country.

"…"

The shadow exuded nothing but silence. It did not even seem to be alive.

When the man that exited the convenience store caught sight of the shadow, his face crinkled with joy and besotted affection.

"Hey! Celty! Were you waiting long?"

"What do you mean? That wasn't even three minutes. Anyway, did they have eggs and milk?"

"They did! I got a four-pack of eggs for now." The man chuckled, holding up a plastic bag.

He had called the strange woman in the black riding suit and Hawaiian shirt Celty, but when she replied, she did not speak out loud. She communicated by typing her message into her smartphone.

"I made sure to clean out the refrigerator before we left. Will that be enough?"

"I don't think we'll have a problem for now, since I can eat all the souvenir foods we picked up. But if you want to whip up some homemade crab omelet, I'd be happy to let those souvenirs rot!"

"That would be a waste. Apologize to the people who made them."

"Fine! Then I'll eat them after they've gone bad!" the man said, his eyes sparkling.

Celty's shoulders heaved. *"Then what would be the point?"*

It was a gesture meant to evoke a heavy sigh, except that she was not actually breathing.

"So, uh, should I put the milk and eggs in the sidecar?"

"No, it's already stuffed. I don't want the eggs to fall over and break," she said and opened the face cover on her helmet—revealing an empty space inside. She stuffed the convenience store bag into the extra room there.

"There, that should work," she typed, once the cover was back in place.

The man, Shinra Kishitani, gave her a warm smile.

"Perfect. Celty, you've completely moved past caring that you don't have a head anymore."

♂♀

Celty Sturluson was not human.

She was a type of fairy commonly known as a dullahan, found from Scotland to Ireland—a being that visits the homes of those close to death to inform them of their impending mortality.

The dullahan carried its own severed head under its arm, rode on a two-wheeled carriage called a Cóiste Bodhar pulled by a headless horse, and approached the homes of the soon to die.

Anyone foolish enough to open the door was drenched with a basin full of blood. Thus, the dullahan, like the banshee, made its name as a herald of ill fortune throughout European folklore.

But that was all in the past.

For now, she led a simple life as an urban legend—and as a woman in love with a man named Shinra Kishitani.

That was the Headless Rider of Ikebukuro, Celty Sturluson, in a nutshell.

♂♀

Kawagoe Highway

A strange motorcycle rode the night streets.

It slid along the ground without any engine noise whatsoever, pitch-black, with no headlights and no license plate.

Celty's trusty steed, the headless horse Shooter, took the form of a two-wheeled motorcycle to fit into modern society.

There was a large sidecar attached to it, stuffed with folk art, local specialties, and even items like pennants and wooden swords. With her ability to freely control the shadow that had a mass of its own, forming a pitch-black sidecar to attach to her horse was no trouble at all.

But without the space to hold another person anymore, she and her passenger had to ride down the highway in the classic two-seater fashion.

If I turned him into a carriage, this would probably be easier...but I don't want to do that. If I draw too much attention, that monster will come after me again, she thought ironically.

She was recalling the face of a fearsome traffic cop who rode a white police motorcycle.

I have to say, though...

The pulse of Shinra against her back as he clung to her made the headless woman smile inside her heart.

Riding two at a time isn't so bad.

Celty and Shinra made a living in Ikebukuro as a courier and a black market doctor.

Until half a year ago when they apologized to their clients and went on a long, long vacation for some traveling.

It was a meandering journey all over Japan that took them six months.

Once a year had passed since the conclusion of her long, long quest to track down her head, Celty decided that if she was going to live in this country in perpetuity, she might as well learn more about it. So the pair went traveling.

Today was the day they finally returned to Ikebukuro.

That was such an enjoyable trip. Maybe it's because I was with Shinra. Or would it have been more relaxing if I was traveling alone? Either way is fine, I guess, she thought, reflecting on the memories. *The snow festival in Hokkaido was great, and the Kerama Islands in Okinawa were beautiful. Shimane Prefecture was wonderful in October. The Izumo-taisha shrine was packed. Oh, and touring the different hot springs in Tohoku was amazing.*

If she weren't completely headless, she would have a vacant, day-dreaming smile on her face right now.

Celty drove down Kawagoe Highway, savoring the mixture of

sadness that their journey was over and relief that she was among familiar scenery once again.

Traveling down a number of back alleys to remain out of sight, she brought them to the rear entrance of their apartment building along the highway.

They had returned to their soul nest, the place Celty and Shinra called home, for the first time in half a year.

♂♀

Shinra's apartment building—basement parking garage

Celty stopped the motorcycle in the parking garage, and she and Shinra slowly hopped off.

"*Ahhh, we're finally back. It's fun being on the trip, but it's actually relaxing when you're back home,*" she said, rubbing Shooter's back, now that he had returned to horse form.

Shinra, however, was giddy enough to belie the rigors of their long trip.

"As long as I'm with you, *everywhere* is fun and relaxing! Er, sorry, I guess it's not relaxing. After all, I've never, ever been relaxed in your lovely presegg-egg-egg-egg!"

"*Don't try to use this opportunity to cop a feel.*"

The conversation was very much in character for this pair—but then a third voice entered the scene.

"Ahem...I hate to interrupt your flirting."

Shinra and Celty flinched and turned in the direction of the voice.

Hiding among the darkness of the garage was a person they both knew well.

"Mr. Shiki?! What are you doing here?"

It was a lieutenant of the Awakusu-kai who made use of both their services.

"Well...I got word from one of the young fellas that the Headless Rider was seen at a convenience store. Just thought I would drop by to say hello."

"*Oh, I see. Thank you for visiting!*" Celty typed into her smartphone, politely confused.

"Hmm, I thought you used a PDA for typing..."

"Yes, but I bought this to try it out, and it's quite easy to use. I learned how to charge static electricity in my shadow and use it to tap the touch screen."

"...Seems very clever, if you ask me," said Shiki. He gave Celty a piercing look. "You, on the other hand..."

Celty was wearing an Aloha shirt and a flower lei over her riding suit, as though she'd just come back from Hawaii. In the sidecar, which had separated itself from the headless horse, an assortment of goodies and souvenirs from all over the country was packed into every inch of space. It was the luggage of the most naive rube of a tourist.

"...You don't seem like you're aware."

"?"

"Aware of what?" asked Shinra. The couple was confused.

Shiki exhaled. "Were you online at all on your vacation?"

"No? It was a vacation with just me and Celty, so we put the worries of the world behind us and shared each other's company."

"At most, we searched for local information at places we went sightseeing."

At that, Shiki understood their cluelessness. "Well, it'd probably be easier for you to check it out for yourselves rather than have me explain it to you."

"?"

"Go back to your place, eat something, unpack, and relax, and then do an online search for 'Headless Rider.' Narrow the results down to recent hits," Shiki suggested and turned his back on the pair. "We won't have time for a proper chat tonight, so I'll return tomorrow. I'll give you a call first. Don't pretend you're not home, Dr. Kishitani."

Apparently, Shinra had been refusing to answer any calls from business clients. With that warning in place, Shiki left the garage.

As he went, Celty and Shinra could only tilt their heads and shoulders with curiosity.

And thirty minutes later, when they were back in their penthouse apartment, Celty had looked herself up on the Internet, and her scream raged across the screen of her smartphone.

"Aaaaaah! I'm done for! It's all over!"

She typed the message repeatedly, incessantly, rolling around on the floor and throwing her limbs about with abandon.

"Calm down, Celty! It's fine, you're fine, you can still make it!"

"Make it where?!"

"I would go anywhere with you, Celty! Into the flames, under the water, into a black hole!"

"I don't want to go there!" she snapped. All the while, she had her hands clutched to her helmet, rolling back and forth.

The facts she found online were shocking.

There was a string of disappearances happening in Ikebukuro, and a rumor that the Headless Rider was responsible had spread so widely that people treated it as gospel truth.

On an Ikebukuro-centric news site, there were a number of articles breathlessly asking, "Is the Headless Rider our serial kidnapper?!" It was even getting picked up by some national news websites.

"Blame the awful Headless Rider"

"The Headless Rider is child-kidnapping scum"

"Imagine not having a head in today's economy lmao"

These thread titles and comments appeared on message boards and social media networks, whether posted anonymously or not. On the most famous site for questions and answers, the queries were pouring in: "My daughter is interested in the Headless Rider. Should I kill her before she goes and gets herself kidnapped?"

"Aaaaah! It's all over. I don't care about myself. But if any of this comes back on you for living with me, Shinra, then aaaaahhh!"

"I don't know… The haters on the Internet don't even have our address, so I wouldn't be as worried about them. I'd be more worried about people we've worked with in the past, like the Awakusu-kai and such, right?"

"No, it's not going to stop at this! They're going to find my background and pin down my identity, then call the school and get me expelled, and the cops will come and demand reparations, and aaaaah!"

"But, Celty, you don't even go to school! I've never seen you so out of sorts before!" Shinra lamented, but he couldn't keep a smirk from appearing. "You really are a resident of the online world."

"It's not funny! I'm innocent! I'm innocent!"

"Hmm. This Ikebukuro forum post about criticizing the Headless

Rider's traffic infractions has got you nailed pretty bad, though. There's no arguing against that."

"Awww... B-but Shooter's not a motorcycle. He's a horse...," she typed, refusing to meet Shinra's eye. *"Th-the point is, I haven't kidnapped anyone! It's true; you gotta believe me!"*

"You're fine, Celty! Believe *me*!"

"Shinra..."

"You could be a kidnapper—hell, you could be a serial killer, and I would still love you just the same!" he insisted forcefully. Celty grabbed his collar with a tendril of shadow and dragged him along the ground, shaking him.

"If I did any of that, don't love me—stop me! I mean, I didn't! I haven't done anything like that! Believe me, Shinra!"

"Uh, Celty, I don't have to believe you. I was with you at every moment for the last six months," he said calmly, despite the constant shaking.

Celty came to her senses. *"Oh! Right! I was with you, Shinra! I have an alibi! In fact, we could get statements from the people at the inns and stuff..."*

"Well...even if we could establish your alibi, where would we publicize it? That's the problem."

"Oh."

"And if we argued our case online, it would just turn into a mob against us, I bet. The Headless Rider posting on the Internet? Is it a sock puppet? An attempt at gaining publicity? Even if they believe you're you, they'd say, 'Why would I believe the story of someone who regularly breaks traffic laws?'" Shinra pointed out calmly and rationally.

"B-but why are they acting like I'm just guilty, right from the start...? Do the people running these sites have a personal grudge against me?"

"Listen, Celty. These tabloid sites that dig up and spread rumors make their money from advertisements, so they want as many views as possible. In that sense, they don't care if their information is true or false. So it doesn't matter how unreliable their info is; they'll puff it up into the most sensational headline possible in order to drum up views."

"Ugh... S-so if they find out it's fake, will the articles get deleted?"

"Even if it's fake, and it causes controversy, that just means a bunch of people are coming to the site to scream, 'This is fake! Shut it down!' which means more views, so they win either way. If they put up an apology after it blows up, then they get a bunch more people coming to read the apology. They don't all work that way...but take this *Ike-New!* site, for example. They've been infamous for those problems, even before we went on vacation."

Shinra was looking at the laptop computer Celty had open. The website *IkeNew!* was displayed on the screen.

IkeNew! was a news website that focused on Ikebukuro.

It was infamous for trafficking in lots of false rumors and inflammatory articles, prompting people to read only the headlines and share them on social media, where they would go viral and start a vicious cycle of bad information.

It was bad enough that people said a majority of fake news in Ikebukuro came from this one site. But every now and then, they broke a big story before the media did, so they had garnered a certain kind of grudging respect.

"Is...is that true?"

"Yep. I hear they work with other sites and buy up the rights to stories. Basically, they've got the worst reputation of any news source in Ikebukuro. But the people who believe their stories will do so without any skepticism. You know, like the kind of people who will assume that stories from obvious satire websites are completely true and share them as if they're real."

"Oh no..."

"...But in your case, Celty, you're already known for being chased around by the traffic officers, so I'm sure most of the people just assume that you would also probably kidnap people," he noted sadly.

Celty trembled. *"Wh-what should I do...?"*

Shinra placed a hand on her shoulder and offered a suggestion.

"Well, if there is undeniable proof of your innocence...and the revelation of a sensational, shocking truth, I'm sure the suspicions people have about you will clear."

"So...what does that mean, actually?"

"It's simple. The real kidnapper needs to be caught and plastered all over the news."

"*Ah, I see.*"

Celty was finally starting to calm down. Shinra gave her a reassuring smile and elaborated on his suggestion.

"On top of that, if it's the Headless Rider herself who captures the culprit…that would have the greatest effect."

♂♀

Takadanobaba—apartment building

"Uh-huh. So the Headless Rider is back," murmured Kuon Kotonami from the roof of his building.

There was a smartphone in his hand displaying an article from *Ike-New!* titled, "Headless Rider witnessed for first time in half a year! New developments in the disappearances?!"

Once he had absorbed the information within, he gazed upon the night around him. Eventually, he broke into chuckles.

"Well, well, what timing… This is gonna be wild. Very wild, indeed."

He was looking at the Sunshine building of Ikebukuro. The lights of the high-rise rose against the dark of night.

"The circumstances are so ripe for intrigue, yet the majority of people don't even realize it—what does it all mean?"

The smile vanished from his face. His grip on the phone tightened.

"They're all so boring. Most of the people in this city only react the way I expect them to react. Only a tiny handful will actually do something outside of my expectations for them."

His eyes narrowed with irritation.

"Headless Rider…I just hope you're not as boring as the rest."

He turned back to his phone. Based on the reactions on the news blogs, everyone was obsessed with the return of the Headless Rider: hollering, whooping, bashing.

Kuon found their reactions to be uniformly boring.

"Hmph. They're all so normal. The same as always," he said, sighing. The look in his eyes was almost freakishly cold and cruel. His words spilled into the night.

"This is why I *hate* humanity."

The expression he wore was far more chilling than anything he ever exhibited at school.

"I can't believe there's an info broker who would actually say that he loves them."

INTERMEDIATE CHAPTER

INTERMEDIATE CHAPTER
The Dropout

Raira Academy—the next day

When she saw Yahiro showing up to school with his face bruised, Himeka approached and asked, "What happened to you…?"

He rubbed his cheek through the large bandage covering it and said, "Oh, I fell down the stairs."

"Are you all right?"

Though her face had a very narrow range of expression, she did seem to be concerned for him. Happy to be receiving this kind of attention, Yahiro felt himself blushing just a little.

"Yeah, I didn't break any bones."

"…You didn't…get yourself into danger by looking for the Headless Rider, did you?"

"Oh no, it wasn't like that at all."

He wasn't lying.

It wasn't *completely* unrelated, but he could safely say that it did not happen because he was looking for the Headless Rider.

"Oh…well, be careful."

"Thanks, I will."

"?"

She was confused by his odd cheeriness, but she didn't seem to be interested in pushing him for more information about his injuries.

"   "
...
"   "
...

There was an awkward silence where neither of them could come up with anything to say. The moment was broken when Kuon was next to enter the classroom.

"Yo! How ya doin'?" the green-haired boy called out, all cheer. He did not wait for an answer. "Hey, did you hear? They say the Headless Rider came back to town last night!"

"!"

"...!"

"Oops, let me make it clear that I wasn't investigating the Headless Rider on my own. It was an article on a news blog, and people were talking about it on Twittia," Kuon insisted, making excuses for himself. Himeka didn't blame him, though. She looked upset, actually.

Yahiro took it upon himself to change the subject from the Headless Rider.

"Oh, uh, by the way, I was thinking of buying a TV or radio to put in my apartment. Do you know of a cheap place to buy those nearby?"

"Huh? Didn't they give you the place to stay in? Is it not furnished?"

"I mean...yes, I'm borrowing a room from them, but it's an entire apartment, so..."

Himeka looked up, remembering something. "Actually, there's a secondhand store near my house called Sonohara-dou..."

"Secondhand store?"

"They were closed for forever, but they just remodeled and reopened last month. The building was for sale, but they couldn't find a buyer, so they had to open the business again. From what I remember, they had an old radio made of wood on display. But the display case also has a bunch of strange things in it, like old katanas and strange vases... I think a girl who graduated from this school is the one running it."

"Oooh... Maybe not the right place to find a TV, but it sounds interesting."

Kuon reacted as well. "A graduate of our school? Nice, very nice. Maybe she can tell us the school's urban legends or let us know about blackmail material for the teachers. Why don't we go there after school today?"

"You can't just decide that for us," Yahiro protested, not ready to jump into Kuon's idea.

But Himeka simply said, "Okay."

"Huh?"

"I feel like I need to explain myself about the Headless Rider to you two in more detail anyway..."

"Really? Then it's a plan!" Kuon exclaimed, slapping a fist into his palm.

Yahiro stammered, "B-but I still have library committee duties after school today..."

And even beyond that, he didn't want to drag Himeka into something she wasn't wild about.

But she replied, "That's fine. We'll wait until you're done."

The three officially had plans to meet up after school.

♂♀

After school—eighth floor of Raira Academy, in the library

"I just don't know... I hope she's not doing this against her better judgment...," Yahiro murmured to himself as he sorted newly acquired books for the library.

One of the older students called out, "Hey, Mizuchi."

"Yes? What is it?"

He turned, expecting to be told to do a new task. The other student pointed toward the door to the librarians' room.

"The library chairman wants to see you. He's got something to talk about."

♂♀

Locker entrance—thirty minutes later

"Sorry, sorry. Sorry I'm late."

Yahiro rushed over, where Kuon and Himeka had already put away their school slippers and replaced them with their own shoes.

"I guess you got held up by a lot of work, huh? Is there that much stuff to do?" Kuon asked with curiosity. He didn't seem that upset about the wait.

"Yeah, the tasks were easy, but I had to talk to the library chairman."

"Library chairman?" Himeka repeated.

Yahiro nodded. "Yeah…we talked about a bunch of stuff. He also gave me his e-mail address."

"Oh yeah? What is this, like the start of your grooming to be the next chairman?"

"No way. It's only my second day on the committee," Yahiro said, as he slipped his feet into his shoes.

"That chairman is very mature, isn't he?" Himeka said. "He always seems to be above everything."

"That's right. He certainly feels like a chairman," Yahiro agreed.

Kuon interjected, "Oh, actually, he really *is* older than the rest of us."

"Huh?"

"?"

Yahiro and Himeka looked at him for further explanation, which he delivered without much fanfare.

"Apparently, he got hurt really bad and spent some time in the hospital. So he's actually repeating a grade."

♂♀

Eighth floor of Raira Academy, in the library

"Um, excuse me, Ryuugamine, where should we put the library committee bulletin stockpile?" asked a younger student.

He turned around and answered, "Oh, I'll take it to the librarians' room. Thank you."

"Yes, sir!"

Once the younger student was gone, the library committee chairman, Mikado Ryuugamine, stared out the window at the front gate of the school.

The boy he'd talked with a moment ago was heading out into the neighborhood with another boy and girl who seemed to be his friends.

The sight brought a memory to Mikado's mind.

A memory of walking through Ikebukuro with a boy and girl just like them, three years ago.

The young man had once rushed through the bustle of Ikebukuro.

He'd gotten involved in a number of events, sometimes causing them himself, and sank into the abnormal side of the city.

"Yahiro Mizuchi..."

Thanks to those experiences, Mikado got information of various kinds faster than most people in the area.

"Amazing. He actually held his own in a fight against Shizuo Heiwajima."

A boy who had come to Ikebukuro looking for the Headless Rider and gotten into a brawl with Shizuo Heiwajima. A string of disappearances happening around the area. The return of the Headless Rider.

Despite returning to the patterns of normal life, he heard information like these tidbits before anyone else.

But all he did was offer that new student some advice. He did not try to form a strong connection to the new urban legend in the process of being created.

He knew that he was a dropout, someone who had left the abnormal side of the city behind.

Mikado thought of his girlfriend who had already graduated and his friend who quit school to get a job—and gazed down at the new students who were getting themselves involved in the urban legend of the Headless Rider.

He smiled as they left the school gate and murmured, "Welcome to Ikebukuro. Let's just hope that...something good comes of it."

Then the shadows of Ikebukuro stirred into motion again.

Both old, stale and fresh, and new air mingled, creating a new breeze.

Even the city did not know what that gust would bring.

TO BE CONTINUED DURARARA!! SH×2
©2014 Ryohgo Narita

CAST

Yahiro Mizuchi
Kuon Kotonami
Himeka Tatsugami

Aoba Kuronuma

Kururi Orihara
Mairu Orihara

Akane Awakusu
Mikage Sharaku

Jirou Togusa
Saburo Togusa

Shizuo Heiwajima

Celty Sturluson
Shinra Kishitani

Mikado Ryuugamine

AFTERWORD

So here we are with a new *Durarara!!* series, titled *Durarara!! SH*.

This story is meant to be a two parter with the next volume, but after that, I think I'll be breaking with my usual *Durarara!!* format by having each single book be a self-contained story, like a series of short works. I hope you enjoy the world of *Durarara!!* unfolding in a new way that's a little bit different from before.

The three new characters I've introduced are each eccentric in their own way. Since they're taking over from the cast of the original series, I've been puzzling over (and sometimes enjoying) how I can get you to love and hate them like I did for the old cast.

Yahiro Mizuchi, Himeka Tatsugami, Kuon Kotonami—each of their names has a reason behind it, which I intend to explain in these afterwords going forward. (If you live in the Tohoku area, particularly around Akita, you'll probably figure it out right away.)

I will leave it up to you readers whether this series becomes the unnecessary snake legs of the *Durarara!!* story or if it becomes snake hands that evolve into a dragon instead. I'll do my best to push us in the latter direction, so please stick around to see how it turns out!

(Incidentally, I consider the *SH* to stand for "Snake Hands," but you could consider it to be any acronym that fits, like "Super-Hard" or "Sonohara's Horny," or whatever you want. Find your meaning and keep it close!)

Now…in the meantime, as you probably know already from various sources, it's been announced that the *Durarara!!* anime series is getting a continuation!!

Yes…as a matter of fact, this project has been in the works for several years; I won't say how many. But that was just how long it took to lock down the same wonderful staff and cast that came together for the first *Durarara!!* series… In other words, I'm overjoyed that the same directors, writers, animators, and cast members will be returning to bring you a new *Durarara!!* anime.

The only reason we're getting a second series is because of your incredible support for the first anime. All you fans out there who stayed fans as the years went on and continued to ask, "Where's *DRRR*, season two?" I am so sorry I wasn't able to be open with you until now. Thank you for your support!

I'm not sure how much I'm allowed to say about it at this point, so I'll just tell you that it will be incredible! I'll do my best to make things exciting on the writing side. Hope you check out the continued anime series as well as *Durarara!! SH*.

Although I couldn't say why in the afterword of *Durarara!!* Vol. 13, this anime series is why I ended up going back-to-back with *Durarara!!* rather than alternating with *Vamp!* or *Baccano!* It's also the tenth anniversary of the series, so there are various projects in the works.

We're doing a collaboration with Morinaga's famous Dars chocolate bar, uploading something to *Niconico Novels*, porting the video game to the PlayStation Vita, and other things I can't talk about here. Suffice it to say that you'll be able to see *Durarara!!* in new forms you've never experienced before. Look forward to it, *DRRR* fans!

On top of that, this has been a year of great change for me, too.

Although I don't know if it will still be running by the time this book comes out, I got the chance to try writing a story in a weekly magazine at a different publisher. It was disorienting getting used to a writing logic that was completely at odds with a novel, but regardless of how it turns out, I hope to utilize the lessons I learned from the experience. If the series is still running when this book comes out, check it out, and if you like it, add it to your list of things to support, in addition to my Dengeki Bunko book series!

There may or may not be other things happening as well, but I'll be doing my best to support all my novel series anyway, including *Durarara!!* In fact, I think that these other experiences brought a new energy to my writing process, because my pace seems to have picked up. Or maybe that's just my imagination…

And lastly, I must deliver my acknowledgments.

To my editor, Papio, and everyone at ASCII Media Works and the printers, I'm sorry for being late on submitting the very first entry of my new series…

To the anime staff and mangaka who are bringing *Durarara!!* to life in different forms of media, between our new anime project and three different manga series.

To the family, friends, authors, and illustrators who support me.

To Suzuhito Yasuda, who provided us with such wonderful illustrations despite his incredibly busy schedule. I love every *Durarara!!* collaboration manga that comes with each disc release of the *Yozakura Quartet* anime!

But most of all, to you all for picking up this new *Durarara!! SH* story.

Thank you, thank you all! I hope that we meet again soon!

March 2014—Ryohgo Narita